Outcrops

Outcrops

Northeastern Ontario Short Stories

edited by
Laurence Steven

Your Scrivener Press

Library and Archives Canada Cataloguing in Publication

Outcrops : Northeastern Ontario short stories / edited by Laurence Steven.

ISBN 1-896350-16-X

1. Short stories, Canadian (English)—Ontario, Northern. 2. Canadian fiction (English)—21st century.

I. Steven, Laurence   II. Title.

PS8329.5.O5O98 2005   C813'.0108971313   C2005-904510-8

Book design: Laurence Steven
Cover design: Chris Evans
Cover photo of Mount Cheminis, courtesy of John Vary

Published by *Your Scrivener Press*
465 Loach's Road,
Sudbury, Ontario, Canada, P3E 2R2
info@yourscrivenerpress.com
www.yourscrivenerpress.com

Acknowledgements

For permission to reprint previously published material grateful acknowledgement is made to the following:

Rick Cooper for "The Pagoda" which first appeared in *The Toronto Star*, June 2, 1991, A10 as the winner of *The Star* Short Story Contest.

Tomson Highway, Random House of Canada Limited, and the Dominion Institute for "Hearts and Flowers" which first appeared in *Our Story: Aboriginal Voices on Canada's Past*, a project initiated by the Dominion Institute and published by Doubleday Canada, a division of Random House of Canada Limited, in 2004.

Heidi Reimer for "Magellan" which first appeared in *Winners Circle 9*, published in 2001 by the Canadian Authors' Association.

Tish P. Sass for "After the Fall Comes Winter" which first appeared in *The Toronto Star*, August 20, 1986, B7 as a "Judges' Choice" in *The Star* Short Story Contest.

Lola Lemire Tostevin and Cormorant Books Inc. for "The Iron Horse" which first appeared in *Frog Moon* by Lola Lemire Tostevin, Cormorant Books, Inc. Toronto, 1994.

CONTENTS

INTRODUCTION

Laurence Steven

The conventional boundaries of Northeastern Ontario—Wawa to Mattawa, Hearst to Gravenhurst, and north to James Bay—reflect a different physical and social environment than what is conventionally called Southern Ontario. The physical environment is demarcated by the Laurentian or Canadian Shield, that gigantic, somewhat saucer-shaped upthrusting of pre-Cambrian granite that stretches from the Northwest Territories through the northern parts of the prairie provinces, sweeps across the northern part of Ontario, through most of Quebec, and into Newfoundland and Labrador. And the social world is shaped in large measure by the physical—the northeast is still an economy dependent to a significant degree on the primary resource industries of mining and forestry, which ship their raw material away (usually south) for processing.

Now, while the boom and bust cycles of such industries continue to plague the smaller communities, over the past generation the region as a whole has managed—perhaps precariously—to break the cycle, developing secondary industries in the mining and forestry supply, equipment, reclamation and support sectors, tertiary industries in tourism, retirement living and healthcare, and even quaternary industries in college and university education and northern research. Such developments are only beginning to register on the Canadian mindscape outside the region. Only recently has Sudbury's world leadership in industrial reclamation and regreening begun to edge aside the image of the moonscape; only recently have Elliot Lake's full service retirement amenities begun to supersede the image of uranium.

Another recognition poised to happen, and for which this volume of *Outcrops: Northeastern Ontario Short Stories* intends to act as a catalyst, is that the Northeast is home to, or has fostered, a distinct English language literary culture, one that over the past generation has tentatively crossed the threshold into regional self-awareness. In 1974 Germaine Warkentin published a fine selection of short fiction called *Stories From Ontario*. Yet, despite her best intentions, all the authors were from southern Ontario, and most were affiliated in one way or another with the University of Toronto. Reading her introduction 31 years later, what is striking is her assumption that the values characterizing Toronto and environs applied equally to the vast human and physical landscape stretching out to the north and west of her. While Warkentin might be forgiven for holding such a view 31 years ago, there is no excuse to hold it now.

Warkentin was following a well-trodden path (or well-paddled canoe route), which had the more northern regions of the province articulated by visitors from the south—with the "south" standing in for the more "civilized" centres of empire. Earlier times recorded the Northeast in explorer journals, missionary reports, and treaty commissioner reports and recommendations. The "northern wilderness" poems of the Confederation Poets for example, and Duncan

Campbell Scott in particular, are inextricably tied to the romantic politics of exploration, colonization and assimilation. Ironically enough, a number of Scott's most famous poems, such as "The Forsaken" and "Night Hymns on Lake Nipigon"—which were published in *New World Lyrics and Ballads* exactly one century ago, in 1905—were written while Scott the treaty commissioner was carrying the reserve-creating and title-extinguishing Treaty Nine to the various Ojibway and Cree bands throughout the region.

From the 20s to the 60s the writers from "away," whether modernist or romantic, tended to see their own predilections reflected in the igneous rock of the Northeast. E. J. Pratt writes his heroic railway epic "Towards the Last Spike" and F. R. Scott twits him by asking "where are the coolies in your poem, Ned?" Yet we could as easily ask of Scott's signature poem, the CCF inflected "Laurentian Shield": "where are the Natives in your poem, Frank?" Earle Birney's self-righteously seeing the INCO smokestacks as "a phallic calvary" spewing "rotten semen" as he drives through Sudbury on his way across the country, is only different in degree from the tiresome bombast of journalists who repeatedly trashed the town after passing through on the train. Britisher Archie Belaney, aka Grey Owl, was able to fool most non-Native Canadians and Europeans because he embodied their fantasy of the noble savage "red Indian." Even in Margaret Atwood's *Surfacing*, the lake and the forest are symbolic mirrors in which the unnamed protagonist from the city sees her past and discovers herself.

What has begun to emerge over roughly the past 30 years, however, is a literature written in English that confidently situates itself in the Northeast, not as a fantasyland, or dark romantic wilderness, but as a home, an assumed foundation out of which the authors explore their human world. F. G. Paci's realistic fiction probing the

Italian-Canadian experience began with *The Italians* in 1978, and much of his work is located in Sault Ste. Marie; Tomson Highway, though originally from northern Manitoba, set *The Rez Sisters* (1986) on a wonderful magically realistic Manitoulin Island reserve; in *Frog Moon* (1994) Lola Lemire Tostevin blurred the boundaries between French Canadian folklore and *bildungsroman* to tell the story of a French girl growing up in Timmins and environs; and in 1996, bringing a certain literary wheel full circle, Armand Garnet Ruffo, a member of the Fox Lake First Nation near Chapleau, published *Grey Owl: The Mystery of Archie Belaney*.

Outcrops pulls these writers together, alongside established names in various localities of the Northeast, and a range of exciting emerging voices. The goal in bringing them under one cover is to stimulate the recognition mentioned above—that there is a literary community in this region, with a distinctive voice. While the recurrent themes are those that characterize all fine mainstream realistic fiction—identity, place, relationships, and home—there are patterns running through the stories that have clearly taken their shape in an northeastern environment: the influence of the resource industries, the close proximity of an uncompromising landscape, the interaction of Native and non-Native cultures, the multicultural mosaic, the love-hate relationship with the south. While as editor I've grouped the stories loosely to reflect some of these patterns, I don't want to pre-determine your response by saying more here. Suffice it to say you have in your hands 20 stories that will surprise you with their quality, delight you with their range, and make you wonder, first, why you didn't know some of these names were Northeasterners, and second, why you haven't heard much about most of these people before now.

Currency Exchange

Colin Hayward

The Winston Street branch was a very old bank, a homely pile of red brick dwarfed by the highrises that blocked the sun on either side of it. On his last visit, Sunath had read the hand-lettered sign in the window announcing that this branch would be closing next month and that all accounts would be transferred to the new outlet opening soon in the Park Plaza Mall.

Sunath had been upset by the news, not only because it would mean a twenty-minute bus ride to put money into his savings account, but also because the little bank was the only one he had ever entered. Back home in Kandy, Sri Lanka, he had never made enough money from his job as a waiter in the Queen's Hotel to open an account. Besides the banks there with their armed guards and identification checks had intimidated him.

Even after he had come to Canada, he had not put his money into a bank until after the theft. All of the money he had saved from his dishwashing job had been stolen from his room. The police had been amused that anyone would hide hard cash under a mattress but the social worker they had sent around had been more sympathetic.

"You must put your money in a bank, Mr. de Silva," Mrs. Hastie had told him, a gentle arm around his shoulder as he wept at his loss. "They will give you a little book to tell you how much money you have in your account. That way, when you have enough saved you can have the bank transfer it directly to a bank in Sri Lanka and your wife can use it to buy her ticket."

He had rolled his head at her in a gesture she did not understand and reluctantly agreed. "All Canadians use banks," she had added as if that clinched it. She could not know that his hesitation was the result of a far more pressing problem.

Mrs. Hastie had taken him to the old bank five minutes walk from his rooming house and patiently explained the procedures. "Any questions?" she had asked afterwards over coffee.

"What if someone steals the little book?" he had asked.

"Don't worry, Mr. de Silva," she had assured him. "The money will still be there. You just go into the bank and tell them you don't have your passbook. Then they'll give you another one."

Thank God they don't have an automatic teller system at Winston Street, Mrs. Hastie told herself as they parted.

Before the theft, Sunath had calculated that within another two months he would have saved enough to bring his wife to Canada. His grief over the loss was compounded by the fact that he had already written to Sita telling her to book the flight for the earliest date she could get. Because of the killings, flights out of Columbo were always fully booked with refugees seeking a better, safer life in countries like Canada. With luck, Sita might be able to book a single seat for two months hence. Since the theft, even if he managed to work two jobs, it would take him almost a year to raise the money again. By now, he knew, she would have taken his advice and sold the few things they owned.

How could he tell her? For the next three weeks, he looked unsuccessfully for a second job and composed letters to his wife that he never sent. One night when he arrived home in the early hours from the restaurant, he found a letter tucked under his door. He opened it and a rush of homesickness overwhelmed him as he stared at the beautiful Sinhalese script, a series of elegant loops originally designed for writing on palm leaves without tearing them.

Sita had indeed sold their possessions and booked the flight. She had used the money to put a down payment on the ticket. "It is very difficult to get a seat these days with all the troubles," she told him. "Many are leaving. A few days ago, Lal disappeared. We fear they have killed him." 'They' might be the JVP rebels or the police, Sunath knew. Either way, his friend Lal's fate was almost certain—a blackened, burned patch of bones and metal tire belts on the side of some road. "Just yesterday, a bomb went off in the bus depot killing seven people. Many others were injured. Your mother was sick that day so I had not gone to work." A wave of fear swept over him at the thought that Sita passed through the depot every day on the way to her job in the market.

Sunath read on with growing desperation. He couldn't tell her to wait for another year. But what to do? Sita would need the money soon. The thought of her enveloped him in loneliness. How fair she was. How fair their children would be, their Canadian children.

* * *

"Taking your break late today, ladies," Jim said.

"Computers are down again," explained Marta, always the garrulous one. "Of course it had to be the day everyone wants to cash their welfare checks. It's madness at the bank, just crazy."

Jim nodded sympathetically. Marta and Agnes had been regular customers ever since he had opened Jim's Donuts four years before. He put down two mugs of coffee on the counter and said, "The Boston creams are very fresh."

"You're trying to ruin our figures," said Marta with a coquettish smile. "I'm game if you are, Agnes."

"Why not? We need our strength after putting up with Bob Gray's complaints all day," Agnes replied. "You'd think it was our fault the computers went down."

They paid and moved over to a window table. "I could kill him sometimes," Marta agreed, "especially that way he has of standing behind you, looking over your shoulder." She shook a package of Sweet 'N Low into her coffee and took a careful bite of her Boston cream.

Agnes eased off her high heels under the table. "Know what he told me yesterday?" she offered. "I was too friendly with the customers. I told him with new immigrants you have to explain things. 'Well the other girls don't seem to take as long,' he said. 'Girls'. My God, you'd think I was eighteen, not retiring next week."

Marta could tell her friend was wound up. "And after you trained him," she sympathized. "Since he got to be assistant manager he's had delusions of grandeur."

"They usually do," said Agnes quietly, looking across at the red brick façade of the bank. "If I'd been a man, I'd probably be retiring with a manager's pension."

"At least you're not moving to the new bank," said Marta leaning over conspiratorially. "The rumour is that they're going to make Gray the manager over there."

"Oh Lord!" sighed Agnes. "I'm glad I'm retiring before I see *that* day." It had been the news of the closing of the Winston Street branch that had made her decide on taking early retirement.

"You're lucky," said Marta. "What are you going to do, when you're retired I mean?"

"Travel," replied Agnes without hesitation.

"Florida?" asked Marta.

"No," replied Agnes. "Somewhere much farther than that. I'd like to see some of the world, have some real adventure in my old age. Maybe I'll see where some of those new immigrants come from. Ted left me a little money when he died. With that and my pension..."

Marta lit a cigarette and they both contemplated deserted beaches under tropical palms for a few moments. "Weather's starting to turn cold. I always begin to dread the winter when the days get short."

Agnes nodded agreement. "You know what I'd really like to see? Elephants. Oh, not like in the zoo. I'd like to see elephants where they live."

"I'd settle for Florida," said Marta, stubbing out her cigarette. "Better get back. Don't want Bob 'Bloody' Gray getting on us because we're late."

* * *

After wrestling with his problem over the weekend, Sunath finally decided to call Mrs. Hastie. She knew how things worked in Canada, he reasoned. Perhaps she would have a solution.

"And your wife has already booked her ticket?" she asked, stalling for time. Really, sometimes she wondered if her clients thought she could walk on water.

Not knowing what other advice to give, she suggested that he go to a travel agent. "Perhaps you can pay them whatever you can afford and they'll let you pay the rest when you're able."

Sunath thanked her profusely and hung up. The next morning he was the first customer at the bank when it opened.

"You want to close your account," queried Marta. Sunath nodded. "Well, Mr…. ah, de Silva, there might be a slight delay. You see we're in the process of transferring all accounts to the new branch."

"You mean I cannot get my money," asked Sunath, stunned.

"Just a minute, I'll punch it up on the computer," she told him. Sunath watched suspiciously as she jabbed a series of buttons. "It's not showing up, Mr. de Silva. Wait here, I'll see what I can do," Marta said and reluctantly went in search of Bob Gray.

She found him in his office contemplating the nameplate on his desk. Although only twenty-eight, Bob Gray worried that his hair was thinning at an alarming rate (to compensate for his thickening waist, Agnes had once remarked wickedly). Only yesterday, he had caught an alarming gleam of scalp in the bathroom mirror.

"Excuse me, Bob," Marta began, "one of our customers wants…"

"Perhaps you could call me Mr. Gray from now on, Marta," he interrupted, putting down the nameplate on the edge of his desk where its legend 'Robert G. Gray' would catch the light. "After all, beginning next week, I will be manager of the new branch." The confirmation of his appointment had arrived the previous afternoon.

Marta approached his desk. "*Mister* Gray," she said with the sketch of a curtsey. "One of our clients wants to close his account. It's not on the computer so I presume it's already been transferred. Can we get it back?"

"Of course, we can get it back," Gray snapped. He wrinkled his nose, smelling the faint odour of cigarette smoke emanating from Marta. "Why does this person want to close his account?" he demanded.

"I don't know," admitted Marta.

Wouldn't look good at head office if people began closing accounts just when he was taking over. "I'll see to it," he said, levering himself from behind his desk as if the weight of the national debt were on his shoulders.

Marta led him to her station. One of the Pakis, Gray thought when he saw Sunath eyeing him anxiously. At least the new branch was in a better socio-economic area. He glanced at the computer before saying loudly, "I understand you wish to close your account with us, Mr. de Silva. May I ask why?"

"I need my money," Sunath blurted out. "Mrs. Hastie said that even if I lost the little book you would give my money. But look, I have the book. Here it is you see."

Gingerly, Robert Gray took the proffered book and, holding the plastic cover delicately between thumb and forefinger, eased it out as if he were defusing a letter bomb. Such a pittance, hardly worth making such a fuss about. Perhaps he would send a memo suggesting a minimum balance of, say, five hundred dollars. Anyway, it was hardly worth punching in his personal code to find the man's few pennies.

"Is this passbook up to date?" he asked suspiciously.

Sunath looked desperately at Marta for guidance. "Have you deposited any money, or taken any out since this last entry?" she asked.

Sunath wobbled his head in apology, a gesture lost on both of his auditors. "You will give me my money?" he pleaded, thinking he would have been wiser to have found a better hiding place.

They'll be letting chimpanzees into the country next, thought Robert G. Gray. In his annoyance, he pushed past Marta and attacked her computer. A minute later he said, "Pay him. Close his account," and stalked off.

* * *

Agnes had taken an early lunch and was sitting contentedly in the reception area at the travel agency down the street from the bank. On her lap lay a pile of brochures describing eons of edens. When the door opened, the gust of cold air around her ankles made her look up at the man who entered. The stranger glanced around nervously. East Indian, she guessed, and shuffled through the pile in search of a pamphlet put out by Air India.

The man was ushered to a desk behind a moveable partition and she forgot about him until she heard his musical accent talking to the agent. So he was from Sri Lanka, she learned. Sri Lanka? Wasn't that where those refugees were from who had arrived in a lifeboat off the east coast. Could he be one of those? Intrigued, she began to eavesdrop on the conversation.

"Yes, your wife's booking is showing for the 25th," the travel agent was saying. "Columbo to Toronto via Amsterdam. Balance owing on the ticket is... Let me see. Ah, $2187. The balance must be paid within three days."

Sunath gasped. So much. So soon. "There is a cheaper flight perhaps?" he asked, dejected.

"Cheaper? I doubt it. Let me just check." A long pause. "Yes, there is." Agnes imagined she heard a sigh of relief. "Mrs. de Silva has booked a one way flight. Total cost $2687. If she had booked a return trip the price would only have been $2487."

"But she is not going back to Sri Lanka," Sunath objected.

The travel agent gave a short laugh. "She wouldn't have to use the other half of her ticket," he explained.

Sunath thought about this. Two flights were cheaper than one flight. The customs of Canada constantly surprised him. "You can get the cheaper ticket?" he asked.

"Sure." A rattle of computer keys. "There. The balance owing after your wife's deposit is now…" a rapid tick, tick, tick. A pocket calculator, guessed Agnes. "$1987."

She heard a crackle of paper followed by the familiar sound of someone counting money. "There's only three hundred and twenty-four dollars here," said the travel agent. Agnes could hear the surprise in his voice.

"Yes," acknowledged Sunath.

A long pause and then the rapid ticking of the calculator again. "I'm afraid I need an additional $1663, Mr. de Silva."

"One thousand six hundred and sixty-three dollars," said Sunath slowly and added with false bravado. " I would like to pay you by the month, isn't it?… I have a job."

"Unfortunately, if the balance is not paid in the next three days, I can't hold the booking," the travel agent explained carefully.

Suddenly Sunath had the solution. "I could perhaps sell the other ticket. After all, as you said, it is worth even more than the return."

The agent laughed. "I'm afraid not," he said. "It doesn't work like that. The other half is useless unless your wife takes the flight herself."

Sunath shook his head in bewilderment, then said in a muted voice, "I must get the money somehow. Thank you. I have three days?"

"Three days," agreed the travel agent.

Agnes stared guiltily at one of the travel pamphlets as Sunath departed. Poor man, she thought, flipping through the bright brochures again. Here he was desperate to bring his wife to the chill winds of Canada while she was searching for a place in the sun. After a few minutes, she approached the reception desk.

"Well, have you been able to decide?" the receptionist

asked pleasantly.

"I wondered if you had any information on Sri Lanka," Agnes said. "It's not mentioned in any of the pamphlets."

"I'll see if we have anything."

"Does it have elephants?" asked Agnes.

"Elephants? I really don't know," admitted the receptionist.

* * *

That night, a Thursday, was Sunath's night off. He cooked himself a plate of curried rice on the hotplate in his room and, resisting the temptation to eat it with his fingers as was the Sinhalese custom, ate it with a fork. After brewing a pot of Ceylon tea, he sat down in front of the small television and watched the news. From time to time, he would mutter some of the lines of the announcers, trying to mimic the local accent but somehow the sing-song inflections would not leave his voice. A reporter appeared standing in front of a bank. Sunath leaned forward. The man was obviously East Indian, perhaps a Tamil but his voice echoed with the dry tones used by Canadians. It can be done, he told himself and then sighed. It was too late for him. The children, though, the children that he and Sita would have, would speak with no trace of accent, would be Canadians.

Kandy with its artificial lake patrolled by pelicans, its Temple of the Tooth, its Perihera parade with elephants and devil dancers, would only be stories to them. They would...

He stopped. Sri Lanka was twelve time zones and $1663 away. It seemed impossible that he would ever see Sita again. Sipping his tea, he tried to concentrate on the news. Someone had robbed the bank in the background and escaped with three thousand dollars...

Three thousand dollars. Sunath found himself carefully listening to the details. When the news was over, Sunath took a piece of airmail paper and carefully wrote a note, in English.

* * *

Sunath wandered around the department store until he stumbled on the toy section. There he found it, a water pistol made of black plastic. Checking to see that he was not being observed, Sunath peered through the window on the front of the package. Did it look like the real thing, he wondered. In Sri Lanka most of the firearms he had seen had been rifles and machineguns toted by the army at the roadside checks. The police had not carried guns, except at night, and luckily they had never come to his house. He compared it with the guns that people shot at each other on television. Yes, it looked the same. $4.98, plus taxes of course. He had just enough.

When he left the store, he took the pistol out of the package and quickly shoved it into his coat pocket. Hunching against the rising wind, he began to walk rapidly towards Winston Street and the old bank that would close its doors for the last time today. Halfway there, he stopped in the shelter of a doorway and fumbled in his pocket. For a few moments, he looked at the picture of himself and Sita on their wedding day. So beautiful she is, he thought. I cannot lose my courage now. He hurried on.

Only a fool would consider robbing his own bank, Sunath had told himself at first. But it was the only one that he had ever entered. Besides he had only been there three times and he had once overheard a man say that they, people from his part of the world, all looked alike. The most important argument, of course, was that he could see no other way to find the money he needed. And he would pay the money back when he could.

* * *

Agnes felt positively light-headed at the thought that this was her last day. Tonight was her retirement party. She knew that Marta had been collecting money for a present although it was supposed to be a secret. Agnes had told Marta all about the trip she had booked to the tropics hoping that she would take the hint. Her spirits were buoyed even more by the news that Robert Gray would not make an appearance today. Apparently he was too busy inspecting his office at the new bank, probably to see whether the throne had been installed in the right place.

Sunath had not expected so many customers so early on a Friday morning. He hesitated at the door and then, with a feeling that his fate was in the hands of the Lord Buddha, entered and joined the line that snaked between the rope barriers.

As the line inched forward as slowly as a python that has swallowed a goat, he checked in his pocket. Yes, there was the note and the gun. Perhaps he should point out to the teller that he was not really a miscreant, that he intended to repay in full the money that he was asking for. No, she would not believe he was serious. She might raise the alarm. The police would surround the bank. They would arrest him, and beat him of course. But not shoot him, that was the American police. He would apologize for the trouble he had caused and explain about his wife. He felt the sweat break out on his palms and his forehead as he realized he was nearing the front of the line.

One of the tellers flicked on her light and the lady in front of him walked off briskly leaving him exposed at the head of the line. Now he even felt a little light-headed, perhaps a touch of the malaria that afflicted him from time to time. Another light winked on but Sunath stayed rooted to the spot.

"It's your turn," the man behind him pointed out.

"I beg your pardon," said Sunath, grinning foolishly. "I am forgetting my little book, isn't it? Would you please honour me by going next."

He stood aside and, with an understandably puzzled glance, the man strode past him and went to Marta's window. Another light blinked on.

Looks as if he's going to his own hanging, thought Agnes as the black man in a worn coat shuffled up to her window. Wordlessly, he passed her a crumpled note. "This is a hold up," she read. "I have a goon. Be pleased to give me $1663."

Good God! All these years at the bank and she was being held up on her last day. Far from being frightened by the man with the timid demeanour, she felt like laughing out loud.

"You have a goon?" she asked.

"A gun," he corrected. "I am not spelling it correctly?"

"And you want..."

"$1663," he said apologetically. "I will repay it when I can. I... I have a job."

The man from Sri Lanka, Agnes realized all at once. That was the exact amount he needed to pay the travel agent. "Let me see the gun," she demanded.

Reluctantly, he wrestled it out of his pocket and put it on the counter between them. "It's plastic," Agnes objected. "A water pistol. It doesn't even look like a real gun."

Sunath shrugged, embarrassed. "It was on sale," was all he could think of to say.

Agnes stifled a smile and glanced quickly around to see if anyone had noticed the drama taking place at her window. No one seemed the least bit interested.

"Put it away," she hissed at him, "and try to look a little less suspicious while I count out the money."

Sunath's face brightened. He watched as she expertly riffled through the notes, put them in an envelope and handed it to him. "Put it in your pocket," she ordered. Sunath did as he was told. "Thank you," he breathed. "I will pay the money back to the bank when I can afford it. I will do it anonymously, of course, because..."

"You will not pay back the bank," Agnes told him sternly. "The bank will never know it's gone." She leaned forward and said more kindly, "Tell your wife, 'Welcome to Canada'."

Sunath did not remember leaving the bank. Outside it was snowing, big flakes that he tried to catch on his tongue.

The next customer handed her a withdrawal slip and then stooped down. "Someone must have dropped this," he said, handing her a small photograph. Agnes stared at the couple dressed in their finery. Behind the pair loomed a Buddhist temple before which stood two elephants. Elephants!

Agnes was still smiling when she punched up Robert G. Gray's personal account and debited it to the amount of $1663.

* * *

"I got another postcard from Agnes today," Marta told Jane as they sipped coffee in the little mall restaurant.

"Where is she now?" asked Jane, Marta's new coffee break companion.

"Here," said Marta, handing her the postcard.

Dear Marta,

It's really hot here but lovely at night. I feel for you now that the snow is there. As you can see from the picture, I visited an elephant orphanage, yesterday. It was wonderful. I even got to

*feed milk to the thirsty little beggars. After breakfast the whole
herd goes down to the river to bathe. The orphanage is near a
beautiful town called Kandy where I have been staying at a nice
old place called the Queen's Hotel. Hope you like working in the
new bank.*

> *Yours truly,*
> *Your friend Agnes*
> *P.S. The luggage you all gave me is holding up beautifully.*

Jane turned the card over and smiled at the baby
elephants standing with their trunks twined together.

"Agnes always liked elephants," Marta observed.

*   *   *

"Tell me again about the elephants," Lal demanded,
fingering the cheap water pistol that had become his most
precious toy.

"Then you must sleep," his mother countered. The child
said nothing. "One morning just after dawn," his mother
began, "I was playing in the garden at the guest house
beside the lake where my mother, your grandmother,
worked as a maid. I was just a little girl, even younger than
you are now. Chandra, the old gardener, was pruning the
bushes and piling the branches next to the hedge. I was
sitting in the shade of one of the kithule trees, watching the
water of the lake sparkling through the trees. Just then, they
came swaying into the garden, three elephants led by their
mahouts. One of them was only a baby. They were from
the temple on the other side of the lake and had come to be
fed, Chandra told me. I watched as the biggest one reached
up with his trunk and pulled down one of the huge jackfruit.
Putting one foot on it, he broke off a piece and ate it with
great delicacy. One of the others, encouraged by his mahout,
began to eat the pile of branches. I was fascinated but a
little afraid.

Then the mahout suggested that I feed the baby. My mother came out and gave me some jaggery toffee. It is made from the sap of the kithule tree and was my favourite sweet. It was the baby elephant's favourite too. As I held it out, he took it with his trunk. So soft, Lal." She paused and then added, "It was the closest I had ever been to an elephant. Before, I had been afraid of them but after sharing my toffee with the baby I realized how gentle they can be."

For a few moments, the child stared at the lacy filigree of frost on the window. "I'd like to meet an elephant," he said at last.

"Next time Daddy has a day off, we'll go to the zoo," his mother promised. "They have elephants there." Then more briskly she said, "Time to sleep."

"One more story," Lal pleaded. "A little one. Then I promise I'll go right to sleep. Tell me the story about the Lord Buddha. You know, the one where he appears to Daddy as a beautiful old lady and gives him the money for you to come here."

Sita laughed. "All right," she agreed. Comforted by the familiarity of the story, Lal was soon asleep. But Sita continued past her joyous reunion with Sunath at the airport to the raising of the temple financed by the Buddhist community. After she had finished, she sat in the semi-darkness gazing at her son, thinking proudly of the $1663 they had contributed to the temple's construction.

As she crept out of the bedroom, she glanced at the frost-rimed window and thought of the monks shivering in their saffron robes at the ceremony to open the new temple. Of course, it was not as impressive as the temple in Kandy which housed the sacred tooth of the Lord Buddha but it was a comforting connection with the past in this chilly land.

She glanced back at her sleeping son. This land was his

land, Sri Lanka only stories. "Someday," she vowed, "he will touch the elephants."

THE PAGODA

Rick Cooper

As soon as he had turned off the red and green sign that said "China Pagoda" and had wearily ascended the metal fire-escape to his room on top of the old square building he owned, Mr. Su wasted no time in sitting quietly in his singlet and lighting a cigarette. The Project, he reflected, had gotten entirely out of hand. He wasn't even sure how it had begun. It was generally known in the town that Mr. Su had a wife, and that his wife lived in China. It had also been generally assumed over the years that he preferred his solitary condition. After all, said the town, Mr. Su was Chinese, and Chinese people never get lonely the way we do, and besides they have their own ways. Mr. Su alone was a simple fact, just as the China Pagoda was a simple fact. And that, up until the last few weeks, had been the most consideration that anyone had bestowed upon the matter.

It was true that Mr. Su had a wife whom he had not seen since 1948. On the other hand, over four decades of separation had not filled him with the kind of anguished yearning that the progenitors of The Project had spontaneously decided that it had. He had come to Canada by himself along with many thousands of his countrymen, and like them his intention had been to carve out a small paddy on the side of the Gold Mountain and then arrange for his wife to join him. He had carved, and she had declined. This had not surprised him. He had heard of it happening often enough, and when it did, the stranded party usually arranged a Canadian marriage with an eligible partner more readily to hand. His wife, Hong Mei, had her family, her village, and her own life. Besides, he had been married to her only a few days before he had left. And now, merely because he had mentioned to some of his customers that he was planning to retire, the town had reacted unpredictably. The Project had been launched, and Hong Mei had been its target.

Mr. Su looked up at the calendar from his wholesaler which was pinned above the arborite kitchen table and noted the circle he had drawn around Thursday which was now only two days away. They were strange these people who surrounded him. Why would they think of doing such a thing? Always unpredictable. Nothing in his life had changed from the day he had started the restaurant, but for them change was like a kind of food, and they were always ravenous. They took jobs out of town; they quit or got fired. They moved house, they traded-in cars, they even changed their women. Women! Mr. Su scraped back the kitchen chair and started to get ready for bed. The women didn't even have the same colour hair from one week to the next. What the hell was Hong Mei going to make of that? And Ellen, the waitress, had moved in with Fred. Nice guy, but both of them married already! Some pagoda!

The next morning at breakfast Fred pressed his plaid belly against the counter and shouted at Mr. Su behind the grill.

"Su ole buddy. Only one day. Then you'll get to poke

one of these." He removed a toothpick from his mouth as he spoke and jabbed it at Ellen's buttock as she swept by with her arms full of plates.

"That's right," said Ellen setting down the plates before some regulars, "Mr. Toothpick." Guffaws issued from the occupants of table three.

"Su don't have nuthin' to worry in that department," observed an intimate of the counter. "Hell, all these years how's he been gettin' by? His reaches all the way to China!"

"Yeah, sure," replied Mr. Su. Strange how these people never seemed to be in a rush in the morning.

BING! Mr. Su hit the bell.

"Two special. Chips and gravy."

"You goin' to the airport, Fred?"

"Nah. Gonna watch it on T.V. Hey, Su!"

"Yeah?"

"Remember my advice on the honeymoon."

"Yeah. Have a nice day, Fred."

"What advice?" inquired the counter.

"Jeesus, listen to Freddie." Ellen punctuated her sentence with a slam of the cash register. "Honeymoon advice from him. It's like goin' to a Shriner for advice on hats."

In the middle of the afternoon on Thursday Mr. Su was shaking hands in front of the China Pagoda with the district councillor and other dignitaries. They started for the airport, and the trip was interesting for Mr. Su because he had not been that far east of the town in years. The width of the highway and the new subdivision which looked like an encampment of enormous tents surprised him.

"You've seen many changes," confirmed the smiling face in the front seat.

"Yeah. A lot."

"It was the least we could do," the smile continued as

the town receded. "Not that hard really. A word in the appropriate ear. A fax or two to...What's that place?"

"Beijing"

"Yes. That's the place."

The principal facts of the case were reviewed *en route* and indeed Mr. Su had been very touched by the tremendous effort the town had made on his behalf. Collection boxes had been assembled and strategically placed. On the advice of the district councillor, the Member of Parliament had been visited and the matter set before her. Mr. Su had eventually met this woman and had had the chance to select one of the pens from her marble desk set to sign the application for the Ministerial Permit. There was to be a dinner at the China Pagoda this very evening although Mr. Su had done most of the cooking for it himself. He had, they had said, worked hard, and the town was going to thank him for it.

In due course the members of the motorcade arrived at the airport and assembled in the cafeteria.

"Go ahead!" urged the councillor. "Have anything." Mr. Su ate a piece of cherry pie and had some tea, a very novel experience since he couldn't recall ever having eaten in someone else's restaurant.

"Do you miss her?"

"Well, it's a long time."

The conversation was desultory. Mr. Su felt unsure of his ground. And as if the confusion within him wasn't enough—the years and years of labour nearly at an end, the strange faces, the even stranger mission, the unfamiliar piece of cherry pie—now, just after the flight had been called, and as he stepped into the arrivals lounge, he was greeted by the intensely hot glare of television lights and young men crouching on either side of him with huge cameras and contorted faces. And there barely visible just beyond the heat and fray, a small, elderly Chinese lady in a rather misshapen brown toque, with a quiet smile, milky jade earrings, and a large string bag.

"Hong Mei?"

"Ah," she said. And he reached forward awkwardly to take her bag.

After the banquet which had confirmed for him that his fellow townspeople were completely unpredictable (the councillor's wife, whom Mr. Su had never set eyes on, had been observed to be weeping volubly) Mr. Su helped Hong Mei up the metal fire-escape. Several times that evening when he had looked across at her he had wondered what had happened to them both, and how it could have been that they had lived their lives in such isolation, and whether, more to the point, this reunion was really for the best. He settled her at the arborite table and began to make some tea. He had to concentrate carefully on the soft tones of her Pearl River valley accent.

"You must be tired, Hong Mei."

"It's no problem, Su. Anyway, I should tell you now so we won't have trouble in the future."

"What's that?"

"Hong Mei died in 1964. You don't remember me. But I remember you...at the wedding. I'm Su Ping. Maybe I'm even a cousin of yours." She chuckled. "Anyway, I like you. I hope you like me too."

"Jesus!" Mr. Su momentarily abandoned his native dialect.

"It's good," she said reaching out to touch him. "Hong Mei was my friend. She would want me to help you. Anyway, too late to change your mind now," she said simply.

Mr. Su lay in bed smoking. Su Ping was already fast asleep beside him. Changes: retiring, closing the Pagoda, his face on T.V. And as if that wasn't enough he was in bed with a woman, and it wasn't even his wife. Enough to make even Fred's head spin. Su looked at the sleeping woman beside him, then reached out and touched her warmth. Fred. What exactly had been his advice about the honeymoon? He butted the cigarette and rolled over against her.

"Goddam it," he said softly. "Now I start to feel like a *real* Canadian."

Red Ochre and Fish Oil

David Burtt

The man paddled the red canoe across the broad, sparkling lake. His wife sat on the floor, reclining on one of the two packs inside. Her legs were extended under the front seat, and she wore only shorts, a sports bra, and her sunglasses. The man wore only his bathing suit and a pair of sunglasses. Their hair was wet, but their skin was dry.

They traveled in contented silence.

At the far end of the lake a pair of red cliffs rose up from the water. The rest of the shoreline was alternately swampy and rocky, and low hills of black spruce forest rose up around the lake. Wispy white clouds were lightly painted on the blue sky like paisley, delicately shifting in the subtle breeze that helped the canoe across the water. The man watched the whirlpools flow from his J-stroke, swallowing the diamonds of sunlight woven in the water. The cliffs grew larger.

The man's wife sat up a little.

"I don't see a campsite yet."

"It must be above those cliffs. I don't think we'll see a campsite, just a place to pull the canoe up."

"See anything like that?"

"I don't know. Maybe at either end of the cliffs. Maybe at one of those breaks running down, where those trees are growing. Let's start at the right side and just work our way across."

The man brought the canoe close to the heavily wooded shore to the right of the cliffs.

"That can't be it."

"The hill's really steep, too."

The man slowly paddled the canoe along the foot of the pink rock wall, listening to the water lap against the granite.

"Looking for pictographs?"

"Yeah. And spiders. There's one." The man pointed with his paddle to a large dock spider sitting still on the rock.

His wife shivered. "I hate spiders."

"I know." The man had a smile in his voice.

"There we go. On the next little outcropping. See 'em?"

"Oh yeah. Good eye."

The man gave a couple of stronger strokes, then dragged his paddle to guide the canoe close to the pictographs.

"Can you get my camera out, hon? The lighting's great right now."

The woman sat up and pivoted to the pack behind her. She shifted it to her left and popped the clips open on the top flap, inner flap, and dry sack. The man's camera sat on top, in a bright yellow pelican case. She passed it back to him.

The man slid his paddle into the canoe, resting it on the thwart in front of him, and proceeded to open the case and take out his camera. He adjusted the lens for a couple of seconds, then snapped three pictures, pausing before each.

"So, Meg, what do think it is?"

"Overall? I'm not sure. This looks like a moose—okay,

two, 'cause here's another one. This looks like a canoe, with a guy in it holding a bow. So I guess it's a hunting story. But I don't get these squiggles over here. But I think, over here, these two things are people. And this might be the sun shining on them. And up over here, in this box, are two more people. Maybe they're dead and on the path of souls—that's why they're apart from the rest."

"The squiggles sorta seem to cut the one image off, like there are two separate pictos. One with the hunter and the moose and the people and the sun, and another with the squiggles and the two people in the box.

"They're all about equally bright. I think it's all the same pictograph. Otherwise why do it so close?"

"Good spot for a picto. Southern exposure, protecting overhang, smooth rock. There are only so many of these places."

The man started to paddle again, moving towards the crevice in the middle of the cliff.

"Looks like an old painter hanging off that tree."

"There's paint on the rocks from dragged canoes. I think this is it. You wanna tie us up and we'll take a look?"

The man brought the canoe close to shore as his wife put on her sport sandals. She stepped carefully into the water, painter in hand, then scrambled up the rocks and tied the rope next to the older painter hanging on the dead, broken branch of a gnarled cedar. Her husband pulled on his sandals. Meg pulled the canoe close to the rocks and held it as her husband stepped out.

"Careful, Darren. These ones are really slippery."

"I know."

The couple climbed up the steep worn path, using large, steady rocks for footholds. At the top was a flat plateau, dotted with stunted jack pines digging in to the rock. The campsite was expansive, reaching from the trail out to the edge of the cliffs on either side and running along them until the cliffs gave way to the wooded slope of the hill. Beyond the site, the dark thick forest was marked by increasingly taller trees growing along the hill.

"This'll do," Darren said with a smile. He pulled his wife to him by her waist and kissed her, his smile still tugging at his puckered lips.

Darren and Meg sat with their legs dangling over the side of the cliff, warming themselves in the sunshine after a half-hour of cliff-jumping and swimming. Behind them, they had staked their claim to the campsite. Their tent was pitched and sleeping bags unrolled, and a pot of water was perched on a burning stove. Their canoe sat overturned near the stove, supported by rocks to serve as a table. The sun was lower on the horizon, but still bright.

Darren warily scanned the sky at the sound of a distant plane. The sound grew louder, and his wife also looked skyward. In an instant the plane flashed in the sunlight, high overhead, flying south. It was swallowed by the sun, then emerged from the burning orb at its side, its silver wings glinting once more in the light. It circled slowly and widely, winding its way down towards the lake.

"Shit," Darren muttered. Meg sat silent, watching.

The plane made its final pass over the west shore of the lake, then disappeared behind Darren and Meg's campsite. They winced at the roar as it approached from behind, low this time. The plane buzzed the campsite, dropping towards the lake as it flew from the cliffs. Darren extended his middle finger towards the back of the plane as it touched down. It slowed, then turned and taxied towards the cliffs, stopping a hundred meters out in the water. A shiny blue canoe was strapped to one pontoon. The pilot stepped out onto the pontoon, ignoring Darren and Meg, then proceeded to untie the canoe and roll it into the water. He sat holding it while the passenger door opened and a middle-aged man stepped down onto the pontoon. He had a grey beard, and wore a plaid shirt and blue jeans, army boots, and a wide-brimmed hat. Somebody passed him a pack from inside the plane, which he placed in the canoe, then another, and another. Then a pair of paddles, and an orange life jacket, which the man quickly put on. A woman, also middle-aged, wearing an outfit not unlike the man's and a lifejacket, stepped out of the plane. She was helped onto the pontoon by the man, who pulled the canoe back to her so that she could climb into the front seat. Then the man pulled the canoe along the pontoon so that he could climb into the back seat. The canoeists waved goodbye to the pilot as they paddled from the plane. The pilot indifferently raised his hand in return as he climbed into the plane.

Darren turned to Meg as the pilot started the plane. "There aren't any other sites around here, are there?"

"Not that I saw on the map. Several kilometers up or downstream."

"Shit. Guess we'll be sharing a site tonight."

"Whatever. It's a big site. We'll get an early start tomorrow. Besides, maybe they'll be really nice."

"Yeah. Hey, maybe they've got some fresh food they'll share."

"Corn on the cob."

"With butter." Darren poked Meg in the side and smiled. The blue canoe came closer.

Behind the canoe, the plane sputtered to life, pivoted, and raced down the lake. It tore from the water with sudden grace, its wings almost flapping for a moment as the plane sought out its equilibrium, climbing up and away from the lake. It disappeared into the sun.

"Hello!" yelled the man in the canoe, raising his paddle in a salute. The woman smiled a greeting.

"Hi," Darren replied, his hand half-heartedly raised. Meg raised hers with polite enthusiasm.

"Can you folks tell us where the nearest site is? We'd been told about the one you're at, but I guess ya beat us to it."

"By our map it's a few kilometers down or up stream. I think the river flows outa here down that way." Darren pointed to his left, where the lake disappeared into a bay.

"Few kilometers ya say? That's a coupla miles, ain't it?"

"Reckon so," replied Darren, sure now that the couple in the canoe were American. Meg stifled a laugh.

The man in the canoe laughed at being exposed. He made no move to paddle away. "How much daylight do you figure we've got left? We're not from around here."

"I don't know. A couple of hours before it gets really dark. But the bugs'll be out as soon as the sun's below the horizon."

"I see." The man and woman in the canoe continued to sit and smile up at Darren and Meg.

"We've got lots of room up here, though, if you want to share for the night," Darren offered.

"Well, we hate to intrude," the man replied, "but I don't see that we really have a choice." He shrugged helplessly.

"C'mon up," said Meg, standing to greet her guests.

Darren followed her lead, then looked to the pot on the camp stove. "You wanna check that pot? I'll go help these people with their stuff." Meg shot him a look. "Unless, of course, you want to get their over-stuffed packs while I make the chili?"

Meg smiled. "No, that's okay. Women's work has its benefits. Just don't make assumptions."

"So you're the delicate sex when it suits you," said

Darren over his shoulder as he walked to the tent to get his sandals.

"Pretty much," Meg replied as she emptied the dehydrated contents of a zip-lock bag into boiling water and began to stir.

Darren walked down the steep trail as the man in the canoe searched for a spot to shore up.

"I think you're gonna hafta get your feet wet," Darren observed.

"Well, you heard the man, Judy. Out ya get."

"Watch it. It's slippery." Darren was both anxious that the woman might fall and shamefully tickled at the prospect. He watched from up the slope without offering more help than his warning.

The woman stepped tentatively out of the canoe onto the slimy rock below the water's surface, about ankle deep. She shifted her weight onto the foot, and began to slide away from shore.

"Oh, crap!" She reached for the canoe.

"Don't, dammit!" the man hollered as the woman grabbed the gunwale.

Darren was petrified—shocked and amused. When he saw that the woman, suddenly over her head, was dragging the canoe out of reach, he sprang into action.

"Let go of the canoe!"

The woman instantly obeyed. Darren ran to the water's edge, then carefully stepped out and offered the woman a hand. She swam a stroke towards him and grabbed it. He helped her onto shore and allowed himself a smile. The man in the canoe awkwardly sculled back to Darren, who held the canoe while he stepped out.

"Wow. Nice canoe. Brand new."

"It's the first time she's touched water," the man said proudly.

"Your packs look new, too," Darren said as he grabbed one and passed it to the man while holding the canoe with his foot.

"Almost everything is," said the man as he struggled to get his heavy pack on.

"I'm Darren. My wife's name is Meg." He extended his hand.

"Bob," said the man, seizing Darren's extended hand in a wrenching grip. "My wife's Judy."

Judy offered an embarrassed smile as she wrung out the bottom of her shirt.

"Pleasure," said Darren. "Now head on up and introduce yourself to Meg. Judy, you wanna grab this small one?"

Bob started slowly up the hill.

"What's in this, anyway?" Darren asked at the sound of rattling plastic as he lifted the pack to pass to Judy.

"Fishing tackle." She smiled.

"All of it?"

"Well, there's the rods and reels too. But it's all fishing gear."

Darren struggled to hide his disbelief. Judy took the pack and started after Bob. Darren tied the new blue canoe off to the dead cedar limb and took the last pack from the canoe. It felt like it was full of rocks.

"You okay?" Judy asked from well up the hill. "That food pack's not light."

"Fine," Darren lied as he jerked the pack onto his shoulders.

His legs burned as he climbed the hill. By the time he reached the top, sweat was dripping off the tip of his nose.

"Not light, is it?" Bob asked, looking winded himself as he reclined on his own pack.

"Not really, no." Darren set the pack down carefully

next to Bob's. "Hope you're not going far."

"We'll see," said Bob. "Hey Jude, pass me that fishing gear, would ya? I gotta catch us some supper."

Judy, still wearing her pack, looked up from the conversation she'd been having with Meg while Meg stirred the chili. "Bob, maybe we should set up the tent first. While it's light out. Besides, I need to get changed. "

"Tons of time for that," Bob scoffed. "Go change in the woods. I bet I'll catch something in no more than ten minutes, right off the face of this cliff. Say, Darren, how's the fishing been?"

"Don't know," Darren replied as he headed to the pot and took the spoon from Meg. "Don't fish."

"Don't fish? Whaddaya mean 'don't fish?' What on earth are ya doin' out here?"

"Camping." Darren smiled at his flip reply as he raised a spoonful of chili to his lips.

Bob shook his head as he took the pack of fishing gear from his wife.

Darren and Meg lay holding one another in the dark blue remnants of light in their tent. They lay in silence, their eyes open, gazing into nothing. Listening.

"Bob! I can't take these mosquitoes any more! Oh, God!"

"Quit your whining, woman! Put on some more deet or go find your bug jacket. Goddamn mosquitoes! Dammit, gimme a hand with this tent!"

"I can't take it! I need my hands to kill the bugs! I can't help you!"

"Are you crying?! Don't you dare cry over some fucking mosquitoes! So help me, if you cry I'll drive ya! Now feed this pole through the tent!"

"How dare you threaten me! How dare you! We wouldn't be in this situation if you'd just set up the tent in the daylight!"

"You shut up! Don't you blame this on me! You coulda set the tent up yourself, woman! Now pass me that other pole. Quit your swatting and get busy!"

"I can't! I can't!"

"What'd I tell you about crying?! I'm serious. I'll drive ya."

"Darren, maybe we should do something."

"He's not serious. He won't do anything with us here. Besides, listen to the bugs out there. We're in here for the night."

"Now tie that line off to that rock. Just wrap it around. Hurry up! God!"

"I'm sorry."

"These Goddamn insects!"

The next day Darren and Meg got up with the sun to the sound of snoring. They packed up their sleeping bags and dressed quietly before getting out of their tent. Bob and Judy's tent stood twenty feet away, awkwardly leaning to one side. Their backpacks lay pell-mell around their tent, clothes and fishing gear protruding.

Darren and Meg felled their tent, packed their packs, and gave the site one last search for any gear that they might be leaving behind. They silently nodded consent to one another. Darren put on a pack, and then quietly pulled their canoe into his lap before hoisting it on to his shoulders. He headed down the hill, followed by Meg carrying her pack and their paddles and life jackets.

As Darren pushed off from shore and slipped into the canoe, a startled loon cried out and then dove. Meg and Darren paddled into the sunlit mist, where the lake disappeared into a bay.

To Shawn:

Best wishes

Barry

26/11/05

The Winning Ticket

Barry Grills

Before all the excitement, it was just a typical day at *Moravia's F ne Italian Foods*. It was mid-afternoon, the lunchtime crowd long departed, too early yet for the kids from the high school, except for four senior girls skipping class who had wandered in at two-thirty for Cokes and chips 'n' gravy. The clock above the fridge, an old-timer with a black hour hand and a chipped minute hand, seemed sympathetic to the laziness of time. Its thin red second hand simply kept on moving, leaping from instant to instant, around a face that said *7-up*.

The people who were present sat in booths clustered at the front of the restaurant, as if they were part of the same group. Many of them were, but not all of them. The ones with the common bond kept looking at the clock.

"The bank closes at three-thirty," Johnny Stephens muttered, shaking his head in frustration.

In his early twenties, he was crammed into a booth with three others who shared his approximate age as well as his impatience. They were waiting for their paycheques so they could temporarily resolve an incestuous economy which bonded them together. They owed each other money.

Johnny was in hock to a short companion sitting directly opposite him, to the tune of thirty bucks. Shorty, as he was called, sported a blonde attempted mustache and, to some people's amusement, had the real name, Dale Evans. Shorty, in turn, owed Randy Carstairs twenty dollars. Randy sat beside him, across from Cindy Irwin, a startlingly obese young woman with a food stain of forgotten origin on the front of her sweatshirt, to whom Randy was indebted for a further twenty bucks. Although she was broke, Cindy, for her part, wasn't as preoccupied with the paycheque which hadn't arrived. Sometimes, when he wasn't being a jerk, she was in love with Randy. He was handsome in a starved or victimized sort of way and he didn't often sit in the same booth with her, so tantalizingly close.

"I hate this," Johnny was saying. "Payday's Friday. Here it is Tuesday. And the bank's gonna close."

Everyone said "yeah" because there wasn't much else to say that hadn't been said already.

Fifteen minutes ago, Randy had gone back to the kitchen to see about the delay. He had reported that Paul Symonds, the restaurant owner, was still working on the cheques and didn't appreciate the interruption.

So the waiting went on and on. A dozen employees now passed the time with coffee and a persistent drumming of their fingers on the scratched and aging Formica tables.

Perhaps a year ago, a former coworker had spread the news that being late with everyone's pay was probably illegal. But no one had paid much attention to him and nothing had ever been done about it. The coworker, his name and face forgotten, had been swallowed up in the anonymity of a larger than average employee turnover.

It wasn't that *Moravia's F ne Italian Foods* was in financial trouble. Not at all. The "i" might be missing from the sign outside, but business was brisk at meal times. Everyone knew Paul Symonds had money. He just paid late. Always had. The coffee, for those who waited, was free of charge, which everyone supposed was a kind of perpetual apology. Outside on this January day, the street was banked with sooty snow. A major storm had hit a week ago. Immediately afterwards, the temperature had climbed and the deep powdery snowflakes had congealed into a dirty stew of sand and salt and litter. Now it was very cold, below zero, and the snowbanks were as hard as granite. Giant icicles hung from the roofs or from signs on the front of the stores along the street. When they fell, as they inevitably would, there would be a loud explosion.

Although the sun shone with that peculiar January brilliance, like an angled laser beam, you couldn't tell from inside the restaurant because the windows at the front were solid with frost, but for a six-inch section near the top of the glass. If you stayed inside long enough, you could forget what the day was like. Then, when someone opened the door, the cold and even a trace of sunshine seemed to burst inside, intent on startling everyone.

Inside it was hot and dry. The furnace, rattling and humming away in a cubbyhole in the basement, spat dusty insistent air through heavy metallic vents. On the ceiling, tired cardboard mobiles danced silently in the breeze, their gold paint aging into a wretched gray.

Moravia's F ne Italian Foods was like an old woman with traces of striking beauty. You suspected it had had a glorious past. At one time, the grimy red carpet had been rich and lush and thick. There was a salad bar in the corner but it had not seen a strip of lettuce in more than five years. It remained at its present location because no one knew what to do with it now that it was no longer in use. Yes, *Moravia's* had once been fancier, known for its fine dining. But now it simply served grub to patrons just looking for a cheap place to eat where they might feel at home. It was busiest at breakfast time. On the wall, near the cart containing the dirty dishes, was a hand-drawn sign promoting the breakfast special. Eggs with bacon or sausage, plus coffee and juice, for only $1.99. And on the tables, there was a full-color cardboard pyramid depicting something called pizza fingers. Someone had attached a white circular label and written "with fries—$2.95."

On this particular Tuesday, there was only one waitress on duty. The kids from the high school called her Happy Hilda because she was miserable by nature. Happy Hilda had now redefined the expression, "slinging hash." It was an integral part of her legend that she could drop a plate of food from a height of three or four inches, and when it clattered on the table, not a single French fry was spilled. Today, Hilda had a cold. An empty Heinz Tomato Juice carton on a shelf behind the bar was already full to overflowing with soiled facial tissues. Suffering, on the verge of complete despair, she dutifully refilled the coffee cups of those who waited to be paid, collected as they were in the front of the restaurant like cattle along a section of fence.

So it was, when the excitement broke out at five after three, there were twenty adults at the front of the restaurant, counting Hilda and her cold. There were the four girls from the high school, two men from a local surveying company, twelve restaurant employees and Calvin Smith, an elderly war veteran who lived in a small apartment on the second floor of *Moravia's*. There was also one child, the daughter of one of the dishwashers. Her mother had given her crayons and she drew colourful little beings on the back of a paper placemat. Her name was Amber, though there was nothing amber about her. Most of us imagine Ambers as tending to be blonde and pretty and slim. This one, five years old, was dark and fat and bearded by the grape jelly sandwiches her mother had served her for lunch

Calvin sat at the bar, nursing a coffee and reading Monday's newspaper because the Tuesday edition wasn't out yet. He drank his coffee a tiny sip at a time, making it last. Calvin's coffee was not free and he had no claim on a paycheque. At fifty cents a cup, he was going to nurse it as long as he could

"Lord Jesus!"

Calvin blurted the words during a lull in the conversation among the group of disgruntled employees.

Everyone turned to look at him.

"Lord Jesus!" he cried again, louder this time, as his body stiffened and he began to emerge from his slouch against the bar.

This time the four high school girls stopped tittering long enough to glance at him too. Dismayed at first, they fell to giggling, then whispering conspiratorially, as if they knew something about Calvin that he would *never* know.

"Whatsamatter, Cal?" Randy asked.

Calvin didn't answer. Frantically, he began to search the pockets of his jacket, the remaining half of a charcoal suit he had owned for fifteen years.

Randy shrugged and everyone went back to what they were doing. Calvin was old and grubby. It seemed to explain a lot.

"*Holy Lord Jesus!*"

"Watch your mouth," Happy Hilda snapped. "This is a restaurant."

That whipped everyone's head around again.

"Look at this," Calvin said to her. "Jesus, tell me I'm not going crazy."

"You're not going crazy, Calvin," Randy whispered to the others in his booth.

Everyone snickered appreciatively.

Against her better judgment, Hilda moved closer. Calvin held a lottery ticket.

"Look at those digits," he said. "Then look at the ones in the paper."

Hilda bent over and squinted at the ticket. "Your thumb is over the numbers," she said. "How can I see if your thumb's in the way?"

"You're looking upside down. Come around here and read it right side up."

They weren't really angry with one another. It was just the excitement. They were getting close to something wonderful and they wanted to raise their voices.

"All right," Hilda was saying. "Hold your horses."

After she came around the bar, she read the numbers again. Several times. And while she did, Calvin watched her face the way a child will look at a parent, awaiting a decision.

"Lord Jesus," Hilda cried in exactly the same way Calvin had just moments before.

"*Lord Jesus!*" They said it together and it came out like a chorus.

Now everyone was up and they clustered around Calvin, squeezing Hilda out of the way, except for the high school girls who watched developments from their booth. Everyone knew Calvin, even the men from the surveying company. It was like a joyful family reunion.

Calvin held the lottery ticket with such determination his thumb and finger ached. When someone reached for it, for a closer look, he couldn't help snatching it out of danger.

Nobody knew who said what, but there was a chaos of conversation.

"Holy shit!"

And "Lord Jesus."

"How much is it worth?"

"A million."

"You sure?"

"Holy shit!"

"Lord Jesus."

And so on.

Paul Symonds, who was in his late thirties and had a prosperous look to him, finally emerged from his office just off the kitchen, clutching everyone's paycheque in his hand. When he figured out what was going on, he hung back for a moment or two, unable to understand a powerful envy that cascaded into his heart. He waited fruitlessly for it to turn out to be a mistake, not yet ready to accept that Calvin Smith, his tenant in the dingy apartment upstairs, was now a very rich man. Calvin Smith a millionaire? It seemed an act of trespassing, a betrayal of right and wrong.

There was still a lot of babbling going on, harmless little arguments.

"If it was me, I'd start spending right now, right this goddamned minute."

"No way. Better to plan it out. Sit down and get organized."

"Fuck that. I wouldn't even wait until I had the cheque."

"Shit, you're a bloody fool. I'd wanna see the cheque. Just in case."

And so on.

Randy Carstairs and Johnny Stephens did most of the talking and felt most of the excitement. They had insinuated themselves into the middle of the fray. They were so close to Calvin they touched him, a touching which had its own exotic excitement, like being first in line to witness the next miracle.

"You should celebrate, Cal," Randy said. "You should do something. Right this minute."

"Leave him alone," Johnny argued. "Let it sink in, for Christ's sake. Give the guy a break."

"C'mon, Cal. If you don't do something, you'll go crazy."

Calvin, though, had grown a little confused. Dozens of thoughts scurried through the tunnels in his mind, bumping into one another and falling down, then getting up again. It took several minutes of concentration before he found the will to act, a way that he could splurge.

"Coffee for everyone," he shouted. "Hilda, the coffee's on me."

Although some people had consumed their share of a small pond of free coffee already, no one really gave it much thought. There was simply too much excitement. Even Hilda, who kept sniffing with her cold, only knew how to grin.

Her boss found the will to speak. "Hilda, the man wants coffee all around."

"Yeah, sure," she said. "Comin' up."

That ended the hubbub of debate. Everyone gazed at Symonds, surprised that he had materialized at last. Now, at least, there was a spokesman, someone in authority who would know what to say. After all, Symonds was a Rotarian. The employees of *Moravia's F ne Italian Foods* waited in anticipation.

"Calvin?" Symonds said, rising to the challenge. "Let me be the first one to congratulate you. I want to be the first to shake your hand."

"Lord Jesus," Calvin murmured, as if, only at this moment, with Paul Symonds wanting to shake his hand, was his good fortune actually real.

When Calvin reached out for the handshake, Symonds transferred the paycheques from his right hand to his left, then firmly did his duty.

There was enthusiastic applause.

Calvin, partially toothless, grinned from ear to ear, and it looked for all the world like a jagged fissure on the face of a cliff.

His job done, Symonds turned to his employees. "I have your cheques," he said, moving forward to hand them out.

People slipped away from Calvin, Hilda to pour twenty coffees, others to collect their cheques, Symonds to read the names. Only Randy and Johnny remained nearby, still touching the man who had been blessed by God, still full of ideas and suggestions.

"The first thing," Johnny said, "is to go up to the drugstore and check the ticket. The numbers are on the wall. That's the first thing."

"C'mon, Man," Randy countered. "It's right there in the newspaper, for Christ's sake."

"No, listen. That's what you've got to do. Make sure of everything. I'll bet it's in the computer. I'll bet, if they feed it to the machine, it'll go off like a fucking siren."

Randy began to grin. "Yeah," he said. "Yeah."

"Whaddyuh say, Cal? Let's go up to the drugstore and blow their minds."

"Lord Jesus," Calvin said, although he was tiring now, finding it all too much to handle.

"We'll go with you. Right, Randy? We wanna see it."

They helped him up from the bar stool, without waiting for his reply. Calvin went along meekly and the three of them headed for the door.

"I've got your cheques, boys," Symonds said.

"We'll get 'em in a few minutes, as soon as we get back," Randy replied, hardly glancing over his shoulder.

They went outside into the cold.

The two young men helped Calvin up the street. It was

less than a block but the sidewalks were slippery. They walked on either side of him, holding his arms, an awkward rhythm to their gait, the imbalance in the gap between their ages. Randy and Johnny wanted to hurry but Calvin was old and stiff. And he'd grown restive, considering he was a millionaire. When his companions decided to cut across the street, Calvin pulled them back, insisting they go to the stoplights where they could cross when the signal turned green.

They caused quite a stir at the drugstore. It was as if their unexplained euphoria was infectious. People grinned at them as they stumbled through the aisles, then laughed when Randy or Johnny laughed.

"C'mon, Cal," Randy urged.

The old man was practically carried, puffing and snorting from the cold and their excitement, across the floor towards the counter where the final verification awaited them. Cal had brought the newspaper from the restaurant, although he had not realized he had until he dropped it as they approached the counter. Randy laughed and stooped to pick it up.

"Here, Cal," he said. "Hold onto it. It's a souvenir now, my man."

The girl behind the counter, mystified by their behavior, regarded them with tired disdain. She chewed a large wad of gum with a vicious intensity, bludgeoning it with jackhammer jaws. She stopped abruptly, though, as Cal and his friends approached. The gum just loitered in her mouth, waiting for the punishment that inevitably would resume.

The girl stood behind the counter, rudely silent.

At first the men were incoherent. The best they could manage was a series of wheezes, their laughter and words cut off by breathlessness, which tried her patience even more.

"Yes?" she said at last.

"Cal," Randy gasped. "Give her the ticket."

Calvin glanced at him in wonder.

"Cal. The ticket, for Christ's sake."

There was a brief, but terrifying moment in which, simultaneously, all three of them feared the ticket was lost. But at last Calvin produced it from his jacket pocket and the girl, with some trepidation, took it from his hand.

"You want me to check it?"

"Jesus," Randy said. "Of course we want you to check it."

The girl began to beat the gum again, really put out this time. She turned to some printouts on the wall and ran a fingernail painted a bright Chinese red down the list of numbers.

Anticipating the result, Johnny gleefully winked at Randy and elbowed Calvin in the ribs.

Bored, the girl turned back to the waiting men. "Not a winner," she said in a rushing monotone

"*What?*"

"Not a winner," the girl repeated with some exasperation.

"Whaddyuh mean, 'not a winner'?" Johnny sputtered.

"It isn't a winning ticket. Okay?"

Randy simply stared. He gazed at the girl and then he stared at Calvin. Calvin gazed back at him but there was nothing notable in the look. He just grinned his jagged grin and didn't seem to understand.

For a moment, Johnny was furious. The girl had made a mistake. Roughly, he snatched the newspaper from under Calvin's arm.

"Look at this, for Christ's sake. Look." He thrust the newspaper at the girl with such vehemence she took a step backwards. "Compare the numbers. You think we're crazy?

Calvin, here, just won the whole bundle."

The girl took the newspaper but held it at arm's length, as if it already had been used for wrapping fish.

"C'mon. Look at it."

At last, she compared the numbers on the ticket with those published by the newspaper.

"See?" Johnny said. "They're the same numbers."

The girl nodded and attacked her gum again. Johnny glanced at Randy. His face kept changing color, from red to white to red again. Calvin continued to wheeze, each breath a cry of pain.

"I don't get it," the girl murmured.

"Check your list again. Maybe you screwed up."

She pulled the newspaper closer, almost touching it with her nose. Finally, an eternity later, she raised baleful eyes to Johnny.

"It's a joke," she said.

"Whaddyuh mean 'a joke'?"

"Someone's changed a number. Here in the newspaper."

"*What*? Lemme see."

The girl put the newspaper on the counter and smoothed it with her hand, the way she might iron a blouse or a dress.

"See? Someone's turned the one into a seven."

"Where?"

"Right here." And she brought a blinding fingernail down on the second number from the right. "Black pen. The ticket doesn't win anything."

As if they were connected to one another, the three men studied the newspaper. Calvin couldn't see anything but Randy and Johnny could. Someone with a black pen and a lot of patience had altered the number all right. Now that it had been pointed out, it was there as plain as day.

"Shit," Johnny murmured.

"Sorry," the girl whispered.

But there was no condolence powerful enough. The three men turned away and headed for the door, silent in their loss.

Outside, they zipped up their jackets and Calvin buttoned the charcoal sports coat he would now have to keep forever. The street was brilliant with an ironic sunshine and people moved to and fro, the way they always did. The three companions, lost in this sameness, could not look at one another. Instead, they stood outside the door a time, trying to digest their loss of luck. Like sour milk, it did not go down well.

"You win some and you lose some," Calvin said finally, purely to have something to say.

Together, Johnny and Randy nodded.

At last they began the long walk back towards *Moravia's F ne Italian Foods*. On the way, much to his shame and surprise, not really understanding why, Johnny began to weep. Whether it was his disappointment or because Calvin seemed almost relieved, he would have been hard-pressed to say.

By the time they got back to the restaurant, the four high school girls and the two men from the surveying company had left. But everyone else was there. They'd had time to get to the bank and they were back, anticipating Calvin's return. Even Paul Symonds had hung around, stationing himself behind the cash register. Loudly, Happy Hilda cleared a table near the back.

There was no need for an explanation. Calvin was no longer a millionaire. It was etched upon his face. Eventually people came forward and Johnny and Randy explained what had happened. There were awkward little gestures of understanding and consolation, pats on the arm, shrugs of sympathy, grunts of empathy.

Finally, after it was all straightened out and everyone knew what had happened, the group began to disperse. Calvin retreated first. It was five or six steps through the snow to the doorway to the stairs which led to his second floor apartment. He moved to leave the restaurant.

Then Symonds got in on the act.

"What about those coffees, Cal?"

Calvin turned, puzzled, not remembering at first the round he had bought the house during that brief, ecstatic time he had been rich.

"The bill's ten-fifty."

Calvin's withered forehead grew deeper furrows of worry. "I haven't got it," he said.

In silence, Symonds glared at the shrinking man.

"Can I owe you till my pension cheque comes in?"

"Doesn't look like I have any choice," Symonds said after a pointed hesitation.

Johnny and Randy and the others stared at the aging carpet under their feet. They felt an intense embarrassment. It didn't quite manage to be anger.

"Thanks, Mr. Symonds," Calvin said, turning to leave the restaurant.

Symonds came out from behind the cash and gave Randy and Johnny their cheques. At that point, everyone began to calm down and things became typical again. There's a comfort in finding your spot and staying there once more. For Randy and Johnny, it was too late to go to the bank. With private inner shrugs, they accepted the fact they would be broke for another day.

As it turned out, before the others left, they divvied up Calvin's bill and paid Symonds what was owed.

After that, in every way, things returned to normal.

Closin' Time

Mansel Robinson

"Death to every green and living thing. Clear the forests, 'doze 'em under, stomp ash and cedar into phone books and post-it notes and bury those too."

My charming, darling husband you're gunned tonight, swilling gin tonight and trying to fluster little sister Sal. Sweet elegant man, your blue shirt untucked and one shoelace loose.

Sal grins, city-skinned and fleet.

"Torch the tree nurseries, pave the rainforest. Napalm the jungle and the old growth and the second growth and the future growth. Agent Orange brought in by the laker-load. Insecticide and pesticide and herbicide brought in by pipeline. Torch the tree-planters. Burn 'em in their tents and in their broke-down buses. Take their pointy little beards and their pointy little shovels and their pointy little high-baller smirks and build a pyre as high as the moon. Let the smoke of bark, leaves and pine cones and the smoke of crotch-rot and the stink and bubble of their stinking patchouli oil, let it all boil and bubble and blacken the sun."

My sister Sal grins again. "Oh, shut up, Bernie. Leave the trees alone. They've never done anything to you but give you a good job with overtime and health care. Quit moaning."

Bernie spews again, instant, but he changes gears so quick I barely hear the tranny shift.

"C'mon, come see. C'mon. We'll put you on the green-chain, on the boardway, you can drink your coffee break sitting on frozen sand under the sawmill, hear that chain clank alive, watch those two-by-fours rolling at you steady as waves, rolling out of the mill, endless, never stopping, infinity. C'mon. Have a taste, have a smell of the hell of forever."

Bernie, Bernie, Bernie. You haven't been on the green-chain since you were eighteen, piling two-by-fours at thirty below. The mill modernized years ago, no more coffee breaks on cold sand— a coffee room with union breaks. Silly, raving boy, you're punching a keyboard now in front of a plasma screen in a button-down shirt.

"Ride with me, me and Frenchy in his Camaro, come home at lunch Monday, Frenchy says, 'well, only four and a half days to go.' Four. Three and a half, three, c'mon, Frenchy in your ear four weeks every month, an earwig, two days to go, one and a half, one, done, see you Monday morning. Twenty years in, only twenty more to a pension, nineteen, eighteen. Seventeen."

And Frenchy dead of a heart attack last year. They buried him in his wedding suit and a Def Leppard t-shirt. Go shoot some pool, Bernie. Cool it.

"I see a tree now, I puke. I'm gonna pave my yard, my garden, interlocking brick, paradise. I die, you bury me at sea, you douse me in gasoline. I want no roots growing through my eyes, through my brain. I don't want any grass on my grave. Blade of grass is just a tree with no guts."

I gotta laugh. Sally laughs too, blows rye through her nose. Not what Bernie wants.

"Funny? Buy a round, funny."

Sal catches the waitress' eye.

"You been a tree-planter, Sal, you carried a shovel and bag, it put you through school, right? So you owe me for twenty years. You think one drink is gonna cover off twenty years? You tree-planters, you high-ballers, brag about planting your four, five hundred seedlings a day. Why don't you stab me in the eye four, five hundred times a day. Stab me in the heart."

She's about to say it. "Quit." She's about to say it. Her mouth puckers for the "Q." A quick kick in the shins. Sal grabs her purse, heads for the toilet.

"Why don't you quit?" is old and ugly country and we're not crossing that terrain tonight. Not on gin and the head gasket shot. Not on gin and tuition for the kids just doubled. Familiar ground, cliché, but not tonight.

I follow her into the ladies. She's in town for just a week so she's packed and ready to run if the good times end early. I want to explain. We talk across the stalls.

"You kicked me."

"Yeah, I'm sorry."

"Why'd you kick me?"

"You know why."

"He's whining. He deserves to be mocked."

Yes, Sal. He's whining. But every morning, five days a week, twenty years, the alarm drills, his eyes say, "that's it, I'm quitting." Every morning, five days, twenty years, he puts on the kettle and makes his lunch. Every morning.

"He wanted to run away and join the circus, he should have done it. Wanted to join the Merchant Marine, go. He's married? Kids to pay for? Tough. His choice."

Yes, yes, Sal, I know all that.

"He's just bugging you, Sal. Hooray for the clear-cut? Pave the rainforest? He's looking for a reaction. Kill a tree-hugger for Jesus. Beluga Margarine. On your case is all."

Or maybe it's regret. He regrets me?
"Friday night, Sal. It's a long life and everybody's tired.
The table's empty when we get back, Bernie's double gin still double in his glass. He's over talking to Dan, the union rep, Dan hunched at the bar, staring at the game. He doesn't look away from the TV, Bernie in his ear. The pitcher lifts his leg, delivers. And Dan flips Bernie the finger.
Bernie sits back down with us. Guzzles his drink.
"What's the matter with Dan?"
"Union fucking rep. Tits on a dinosaur."
"That dinosaur got you your house, Bernie. Got you the good wages to buy you that nice house."
"Any loony-left crap you don't believe, Sal? Christ was a black woman? God's a vegetarian?"
"C'mon, Bernie. Go easy. And you've carried a union card for twenty years. Smarten up."
"Yeah, yeah."
"The band's back on. Wanna dance?"
"Dance with your sister. No doubt she dances with girls. It's the correct thing to do."
"That pickle up your ass has just flowered into a watermelon, Bern. C'mon, Sis. Rock 'n' Roll."
"Blitzkrieg Bop." "Jet Boy, Jet Girl." "Kill The Poor." "London Calling."
Sweating out the week. Shaking it off. Laughing it off. Winning.
"Wild Thing." "What I Like About You."
Sal and I are back at the table again but Bernie stands at the bar beside Dan. Bernie must've switched to rye, his tall glass like a jar of gasoline. I can't hear him, no, but I know him—whatever's going on: snipe, snipe. Dan in a brown leather jacket, shoulders hunched, armoured. Snipe. Snipe. Dan stares at the TV, an easy grounder to third. Snipe. Snipe. Snipe. Dan turns, looks at Bernie. He smiles a smile drained

of everything but twenty years and the shingles need replacing. Dan turns back to the game. Fly ball to center. Bobbled.

Dan walks away. Puts his glass on the nearest table. A wild pitch and Dan doesn't see the punch coming. I close my eyes so I don't see the ones that come after that. I guess it's over quickly. I close my eyes, I close my eyes, I close my eyes and listen to the guitar player walk his fingers up the frets.

Morning.

Bernie cooks breakfast. I take coffee in to Sal in the spare bedroom. She says she's gonna sleep in. She means hide. She asks me if I'm OK. I'm OK.

Bernie bustles around the kitchen, yeah, bustles, happy as a double play. The eggs are greasy, just the way I like them.

"Bacon crisp enough?"

"Are you gonna talk to me?"

"I am talking to you."

"Are you gonna tell me what that was about? You and Dan?"

"Baseball."

"Bullshit."

"He thinks the designated hitter is good for the game."

"I wasn't going to get into it last night 'cause you were drinking."

"I was drinking?"

"But we're going to get into it now. What's up with you and Dan?"

"I heard you were sleeping with him."

"Bernie."

"OK. He called you fat."

"Bernie."

"What?"

"Answer me or I'll fork you. And I mean fork you."

He pauses.

"The mill."

"Yes?"

"Dan lied to me. He lied to us all."

He pauses.

He pours out more HP sauce.

He pauses.

He dips his toast in the yoke.

He pauses.

"What about the mill?"

You don't need to say it.

"They say there's a few t's to cross, i's to dot."

I know already.

"But the layoff notices come out Monday."

I've already guessed.

"And two months from now, we're done for good."

Sal and me, we go dancing Saturday night. *"Mustang Sally."* Devil with the blue dress blue dress blue dress, devil with the blue dress on. The word on the closing is out tonight and the old crowd is out tonight, too. They swing it up, they swing it out. *"Mamma's Got a Squeeze Box." "Peg Leg Peggy."* The dancers cut in close for the honey huggers, *"When A Man Loves A Woman,"* and everyone is hanging on tight tonight, everyone's hanging on. The game's a blowout, no one's watching, everyone's hanging on.

Bernie comes in just at closing time, shaved, showered and sober, his good shirt and his new jeans. He puts his car keys on the bar and Kenny pours him a Crown Royal, neat. He taps the shot glass once on the wood and downs the whisky. He doesn't order another one.

"Piece of My Heart."

Bernie is standing with his back to the bar, leaning back on his elbows to watch me and sister Sal dance the last dance of the night.

"96 tears." " 96 tears." " 96 tears."

WAGES OF SIN ETC.

Vera Constantineau

Susan presses the doorbell and listens to the faint echo of its chime. The door suddenly sweeps wide in front of her, displaying a fifty-something man in loose boxer shorts and a muscle shirt, which clearly shows he has very little muscle to display. The boxers are garish, decorated with a hundred reindeer, each one sporting a fluorescent green wreath around its neck.

"You're not Dora!" he shouts into Susan's face, and slams the door. The Christmas wreath swings back and forth, tiny bells tinkling, then settles into its normal position. Susan closes her mouth and grits her teeth. Her shoulders stiffen and her gaze narrows as she crosses the hall.

She presses another doorbell and steps back half a pace to wait. The homogeneous door opens slightly. A face appears tentatively in the gloom, eyebrows pulled tightly together as if rejection has recently been practiced to enable a smooth and immediate delivery.

"Yes?"

Susan quickly prompts herself: big smile Suse, show lots of teeth. Remember what the district manager said, this is the Christmas season. Everyone buys a lot of this stuff at

Christmas.

"Hi, I'm Susan your Nova Dealer. May I show you my shop?" Susan cheerily waves her product book, careful not to obscure its 10% off banner. "No." The suspicious face disappears once more behind the closed solid wood door. Susan imagines the woman's ear pressed against the door, checking that she has actually departed.

Susan crosses the hall. Before pressing the next doorbell, she pauses to compose herself, inhaling a mixture of cooking smells, potpourri and wet cat. She checks that her holly lapel pin is straight, fixes her smile in place, and reaches, with the slightest hesitation, to ring the doorbell.

The usual muted ti-so followed by the sound of running feet issues eerily from the other side. The door opens. A large woman wearing pink foam curlers looks back at Susan, who momentarily fails to recognize a friendly look.

"Hi." The smile is a bit hard for Susan to maintain while registering that the woman is wearing a semi-sheer nightie that sways against the floor. "I'm Susan, your Nova Dealer." An audible gulp escapes her throat; her voice has risen a full octave during the sales pitch. Susan's desire for a quick firm 'no' followed by a slammed door is palpable. "May I show you my shop?" She gamely raises her product book and waves it back and forth for the woman to see.

"Sure. Just give me a minute, okay?" The woman retreats into her apartment, leaving the door slightly ajar. Susan can hear the scraping sound of someone dragging something heavy across parquet flooring. She looks down the hallway to the beckoning elevator and contemplates escape. At that moment, the woman returns and pulls the door fully open.

"Come on in Honey, I just had to move the boxes out of your path."

Artificial branches of a Christmas tree stick out of a box in the corner and several smaller boxes containing decorations are piled on the couch. Susan wonders if her mother knows about the odd people living in this apartment block, and then thinks she probably does. It would be just like her to make this zoo the training ground.

The woman is standing in a pool of strong afternoon sunlight that shines through the uncurtained patio doors. In this light, Susan can see that the woman is wearing a tank top and spandex pants under her nightie. It's a tremendous relief that the woman is not actually naked. Susan speculates for a moment on the reasons why anyone would dress this way before deciding it makes for altogether too many weird scenarios. The woman nods to the end chair at the dining room table, and Susan sits.

"That's cute Honey, that thing about your shop." The woman considers the book Susan has given her. Then she looks over the top of it at Susan and uses her head to gesture to the far corner of the living room where a computer station is set up. "You might say that is my shop." Beside the obviously expensive high tech monitor on the desk is an office style multi-line telephone with a red light blinking steadily indicating an in-coming call. "Never mind the phone Honey; I can always get the next one." The woman slowly turns the pages of Susan's product book.

Half an hour later Susan leaves with a sixty-dollar order tucked in her bag. She looks back just before closing the door. The woman switches on her stereo and muffled Christmas carols spill into the hallway. Susan sees her reach for the telephone.

"Hello Santa. Have I kept you waiting a long, long time? Shall I tell you what a very, very bad girl I've been?" The woman's voice has changed, now sounding incredibly childlike. She is clutching a fistful of her nightie as she sways back and forth in the sunbeam. She looks toward the door and Susan and mouths a low-pitched 'Bye Honey'.

Susan pulls the door shut; she runs the entire length of the hall to the open elevator. When its sliding doors close, she wraps her arms tightly around herself. Then, knowing she is safe, knowing nobody can see her, she begins to dance in a tight circle as she sings, "I made a sale. I made a sale."

Mabel's Kitchen

Barbara Fletcher MacKay

From long habit, Mabel Boyer got up at five in the morning to do some baking. Her kitchen was centrally heated but cold in the corners so she took paper and kindling and started a fire in the Franklin stove. She made herself a cup of strong tea, sat by the stove in her rocking chair and pulled a quilt over her knees. It was her favourite time of day. She was content living by herself with her bird feeders and her kitchen and an aging dog, Jack, named in honour of her first husband

Both her husbands had worked in the north, subcontracting for pulp and paper companies. When they were gone, she had begun to sell beer and liquor in her kitchen. Men had knocked at her back door after hours to sit and drink. Sometimes they came in the afternoon, or on a Sunday morning, hung over. She was circumspect, so they drank and talked quietly; if they wanted noise and women she had turned them away. She was a big and careful woman and had had no trouble with them. Most had been old friends of her husbands, lumberjacks in town with the spring breakup after a season of cutting wood. She recalled them now because she could hear the creeks running outside the house as the winter snows melted. She finished her tea and set to work. The dog yawned on his bed, then got up and padded around her. She liked to talk to him while she was baking.

She lived in an old frame house on a street full of families near the mouth of a river. The children of the neighbourhood visited her often and she always had something for them: cookies, butter tarts, cupcakes with icing, cinnamon buns. They'd settle in and talk away to her in the kitchen. Prolonging their stay, she knew that.

The sun was up and her baking finished when there was a timid knock on her front door. The two Duggan children from up the street were on her doorstep, pinched and cold. It was a Saturday morning and as usual they had been put out too early to play. Amanda was nearly ten, skinny and imperious, rather like her mother Mabel thought, and Luke was six. He never spoke.

"The doctor says he's half mute," Amanda had told Mabel. "He talks at home and maybe to one friend at school but that's all, so I have to talk for him." Mabel knew that sometimes Amanda put her own words into Luke's mouth.

This morning Amanda was withdrawn and silent. Luke went straight to the dog and knelt down on the floor beside him.

"Sit over there and get warm by the stove," Mabel said to Amanda. "I'll make us cocoa and toast if you like."

"Yes, please, Mrs. Boyer," Amanda replied.

"And Luke? Would he like some?"

Amanda looked down at her brother. He was patting Jack with great concentration and the dog seemed to understand that he was not required to roll over and play.

"Yes," Amanda said. "He would like some too please. And cookies please."

Mabel put plates and jam on the table, mixed dry cocoa

with tablespoons of cold milk and sugar, then set a pan of milk on the stove to heat. She had cut thick slices from one of her white loaves to make toast when there was a hard knock on her back door, as though with a fist. Damn, she thought.

She knew the knock. Gus was her one remaining customer. She hadn't seen him for a long time. He must have spent part of the winter with his daughter, poor girl. She went to the door to tell him that she was busy, but he looked terrible.

"Can I come in for a little while Mabel? It's freezing down at my place."

She could believe that. He lived in a tarpaper shack.

"Well come on in and warm yourself," she said. "I'll make you a hot cup of coffee."

"And a little something in it, please, Mabel." She could see that he had the shakes.

He followed her into the kitchen. Amanda was staring at them and Luke had his head buried in the dog's neck.

"Gus, you go on over to the rocking chair and warm up by the stove. Amanda, Luke, come, we'll have something to eat."

They hurried to the table and sat with their backs to him. She stirred up cocoa in cups, put a full plate of cookies down in front of them and gave them a slice each of buttered toast. They ate without speaking. She made Gus a cup of instant coffee, then went to the back porch and added a double dose of dark rum.

"What's that funny smell?" Amanda asked.

"It's cough medicine. He's not feeling very well."

Amanda and Luke were eating raisin cookies when a knock came at the front door. It was their mother. They heard her speaking to Mabel. "I wonder where my children could be."

Amanda shouted from the kitchen. "We're in here."

Mrs. Duggan went through and was about to speak when she saw Gus half asleep in the rocking chair. Her back stiffened and she moved quickly to her children "Come along you two, it's time to go," she said. "Honestly, you'd think you never had anything to eat at home. Say good-bye and thank you to Mrs. Boyer."

Amanda thanked her as Luke fled outside. She added, "Luke wants to thank you too, Mrs. Boyer."

Mabel was resting in her rocking chair later in the day when Amanda came back on her own.

"Luke wants to know if the police take bootleggers to jail?"

Mabel sighed and shook her head. "Tell Luke the police can't be bothered to take them to jail. They don't cause enough trouble."

Amanda nodded. She left without speaking.

Later that week Mabel met Luke and Amanda coming along the street with their mother. Mrs. Duggan said a curt hello and the children averted their eyes. They did not knock on her front door again. Nor did the other children in the neighbourhood.

It was summertime when Mabel answered a knock at her back door and there was Luke.

"Well Luke, hello. What brings you here?"

For the first time, she heard him speak. "It's nice at your house. Mrs. Boyer, do you have a cookie?"

"Well yes I think I do. Wait here a moment."

She brought two freshly made chocolate chip cookies wrapped in a paper bag and tucked them into his jacket pocket. "Here you go."

"Thank you," he said. "Is Jack home?"

"Yes he is, but he's sound asleep."
"All right," he said. " I'll come tomorrow."
He walked away.
Mabel returned to her kitchen.

THE IRON HORSE

Lola Lemire Tostevin

I rode the iron horse for the first time when we moved from Timmins to St. Bruno on the Quebec side of Lake Temiskaming, when I was seven years old. Everyone called the train the iron horse then because someone was supposed to have misunderstood *le chemin de fer* for *le cheval de fer*. Probably the English, my mother said. When it came to French, the English couldn't put three words together without getting one of them wrong. The English, the main prong in a French Canadian's three-pronged fork.

Whenever my mother told me how she brought her mother's body back to Cochrane on the train from Ottawa, I envisioned a black iron horse, eyes fiery as coals, nostrils smoking, prancing the tracks, clickety-clack, clickety-clack of hoofs on the railway tracks, and my grandmother's body in a wooden box. Clickety-clack, clickety-clack, break your grandma's back.

I don't know how many times I've heard how my grandmother worked herself to death and how that made her an angel. An angel was someone who had borne seven children by the time she was thirty-three, looked after them with next to nothing because her husband was only seventeen himself when he married. His father had taught him carpentry, he was a good cabinet-maker for his age, but after a hard day's work he assumed that he could go out at night, that it was his due. Drinking and "other things", my mother called it, adding furtiveness to the long list of components that went into the making of an angel, her voice resigned because that was what was expected in those days. An angel never complained, worked around the clock, and if she got tired, she went to Monsieur le Curé for guidance. The Clergy, the second prong in our three-pronged fork. I suspect that's why my mother had only one child. No man was going to tell her to bear a child every year, no man wearing a dress was going to tell her how to run her life. Clickety-clack.

We moved from Timmins to live on my great-uncle's farm, *mon oncle* Ti-Roc, on my father's side. He was getting too old to look after things and he promised that my father would inherit the farm if we moved in and helped. We'd just had the phone installed two weeks before and it was as if the offer had come directly from heaven. As good as the money was, diamond drilling at the Hollinger mine, my father said it was too much like being buried alive. He'd come home covered in soot, black as a bug, and tell us about the elevators crashing to the bottom of a shaft or dynamite detonating at the wrong time. Our neighbour had been killed in a cave-in and one of my uncles had almost died in a dynamite blast. He'd spent months in hospital with so many bits of rock embedded in him, his body looked like a crater. For years he had specks of stone coming out of his skin and he would give me a penny for every fragment I could extract. Clickety-clack. All that frontier living was closing in, so my parents decided it was time to move on. They sold everything they owned in Timmins, their four-room house, the furniture, and we set out to sow our seeds of independence.

My father was very excited with what he found: acres of arable land, a large house, a rural setting on the edge of nowhere—in short, paradise. My mother, however, was wary from the beginning. Someone fibbed about snakes in paradise, she would tell friends and family later, "It's roosters that cause all the trouble in paradise, the way they rule over the entire coop," and *mon oncle* Ti-Roc's rooster was particularly vicious. It was my mother's job to feed the chickens but the rooster wouldn't let her near them. That's when she learned the chickens weren't very smart. She tried leaving food on her side of the fence but they wouldn't walk around the fifteen feet of wire open at each end. It was quite a sight, my mother with a bucket of feed in one hand, a broom in the other, and the rooster prancing up and down, his comb cocked two inches on his head, daring anyone to cross the fence, and even if we didn't cross it he'd chase us all the way back to the house. Never stalked men, but hated women. I don't imagine he ever recovered all his feathers. My mother would just as soon have wrung his neck, turned him into a stew, because God knows we needed the food. The only thing he was good for was waking us at dawn every morning, he was an expert at that. Went off like an alarm when it was barely light, the signal for my mother to get up and prepare breakfast for the men, because they worked like horses and would have eaten like horses too if there had been enough food in the house.

We arrived in St. Bruno as I was entering grade two. My mother wanted me to make a good impression on my first day of school and she'd sewn me a brown woollen dress with a row of red apples and smocking across the front. Apples for the teacher and all. I was especially proud of my matching red socks and my red schoolbag. But when several children called on me to walk the new girl to school my mother broke into tears. She'd made a terrible mistake, she said, dressing me up as if we came from the city. The children were mostly in rags, one of them wasn't even wearing shoes, they were poorer than the poorest in our neighbourhood in Timmins. We'd been a little short at times, had taken clothes-hangers to the dry cleaners for a penny apiece, but we'd never wanted for anything as important as shoes. This was not what she'd planned for her daughter.

Poverty mustn't have been a concept I worried about because I don't remember how the children were dressed, but I do remember several of us going to the general store in *mon oncle* Ti-Roc's horse-drawn wagon after school. According to my mother, my uncle had the same temperament as his rooster, and just about as much money. He'd promised to buy whatever food we couldn't raise on the farm and my mother had given him a list of provisions she needed but all we brought back was flour, yeast, sugar, and baloney. He expected my mother to make everything, including her own bread. She'd spent the first week cleaning the farmhouse, scraping hardwood floors, slathering them with wax, buffing them by hand, had hardly complained, but she drew the line at having to make her own bread. "I've never shunned work, but your grandmother made her own bread, shined floors by hand, made our clothes, took in other people's ironing, bore a child every two years, and where did it get her?" Clickety-clack, clickety-clack, break your grandma's back.

There is a photograph of my mother standing in front of her grandfather's shop, Louis Séguin and Son—Sash and Door, the sign in English because that's where the business was, with the English, and you didn't want to offend them by flaunting your French. She is wearing a coat her mother has just made her. There was nothing my grandmother couldn't duplicate from a catalogue, and every spring and fall two of her four daughters received a new coat or dress. If the required material couldn't be purchased that season, coats were turned inside out, recut, details changed here and there, and presto, a new garment was produced. Spring coats were made into winter dresses, winter dresses that showed too much wear were cut up for appliqués or made into collars and buttons for coats, because frugality was another requirement for angelhood. "What did the mother moth say to her baby moth?" my mother would ask me, trying to get me to eat everything on my plate. *Si tu n'manges pas ta gabardine, tu n'auras pas de crêpe de chine.*

"I remember the day that picture was taken, the first time I wore that coat, marvelling at how rich we were," my mother repeats each time we look through the family albums. "We lived above the shop, the largest apartment I'd ever seen, except for those two-story company houses the English lived in, in Iroquois Falls. Everything seemed fine until my mother and I went to Ottawa to consult a heart specialist, and the next thing I knew I was bringing her body back in a box and everything changed after that." Clickety-clack, clickety-clack. "I'm no angel like my mother," she adds, "but I'm no Rose Latulippe either."

For generations, French Canadian fathers, afraid their daughters will dishonour the family, have related various versions of the legend of Rose Latulippe. Woman and her demon's gifts, because the Devil always entered a family's affairs through the female side. The Devil, third prong in our three-pronged fork. "In this respect my family remained pretty faithful to tradition," my mother said. "These myths often covered up what was really going on, but we're not supposed to talk about that."

The widower Latulippe had only one daughter, a

sixteen-year-old whom he adored. My mother, also sixteen when her mother died, was the oldest of three still living at home. While the widower Latulippe catered to his daughter's every wish, my grandfather, distraught with grief, drank and ran around even more than he did before my grandmother died. There were also rumours that he was stealing from his father's shop, and within a few months of my grandmother's death he left his father's business and moved to Timmins with the three children, into a "two-room shack barely fit for pigs, it didn't even have floors."

"Men were very good at pioneering, prospecting, trailblazing, and spending nights at the whorehouse up the hill, but children, that was woman's work, and if the little woman wasn't around it didn't get done," my mother said. "I should have been in school but like most French Canadians I'd not gone back after the elementary grades. There were no French high schools in Timmins or Cochrane, no French high schools in Ontario until 1969. If you'd attended *l'école séparée*, spoke French at home, you couldn't keep up in an English high school, so almost no one made it past grade eight unless they went to *un couvent* or *un collège*." Her ten-year-old sister was sent to a convent but at sixteen my mother was considered old enough to fend for herself. She cleaned house for a well-to-do family for a few weeks but the three sons wouldn't leave her alone. She tried living with her oldest sister and husband but he wouldn't keep his hands to himself either. My uncle could never be trusted around young girls when I was growing up but we're not supposed to talk about that either. Nor are we supposed to talk about my mother getting pregnant a few months after she met my father, and how they married when she was only seventeen.

"I can't tell you what I went through that first year my

mother died. I can't tell you because that's not the kind of
story you pass on to your child. All I can tell you is, my life
changed as abruptly as Rose Latulippe's did when the
widower Latulippe gave a party on the night of Mardi Gras.
As if my mother's death had been the stroke of midnight
that marks Ash Wednesday or Lent."

My mother almost never misses an opportunity to turn
an event into an allegory. Allegories allow her to hint at
things other than what is actually being said. Her memory
becomes so absorbed by the ambiguities of her circuitous
accounts that the facts can be altered any way she wants,
because they are, after all, only incidental details of a story.
Allegories allow her to express her differences, whether
they be with my father or with her past, without having to
clarify the circumstances. Repeating the legend of Rose
Latulippe while dissociating herself from its main character
allows her to warn me against, while differing from, the
moral of the tale.

As hospitable as he was, Latulippe had warned his
guests that on the exact stroke of midnight the merrymaking
must stop. There was a storm of the Devil's making outside,
a terrible wind hurling snow at the shutters of the
widower's beautiful country house. Inside, everyone was
having a wonderful time, especially Rose. She danced every
dance with a different admirer, rather than with her fiancé,
the man her father had picked to be her husband. She did
stop once, though, towards eleven o'clock, when there was
a fierce knocking at the door and Latulippe, after a brief
hesitation, opened it. A young man stood before him, a dark
silhouette against the whiteness behind. He asked politely
if Latulippe would give him shelter since he had lost his
way and, at Latulippe's invitation, he entered in a flurry of
snow.

When the young man removed his fur-lined coat the

guests were astonished at how handsome and elegant he was, dressed in black velvet and cream silk. He refused to part with his dark fur hat or black gloves, undoubtedly the whim of a *seigneur*. With utmost grace he apologized for having interrupted the party and begged the host and guest to carry on with their festivities. One guest, casting a glance through the window, exclaimed, "*Nom du ciel, quel beau cheval!*" Everyone was dumbfounded at the sight of the stranger's mount, black as night, eyes as fierce as glowing coals, without a trace of frost on his magnificent, gleaming coat. Latulippe invited the young *seigneur* to put his horse in the stable but he politely declined. Such small eccentricities in a *seigneur de la ville* only added to his charm. Everyone was anxious when the young man accepted a glass of spirits and suffered a slight convulsion as he swallowed the liquid; no one realized that Latulippe had been short of bottles and had poured some of the *whisky blanc* into a flask that had once held holy water.

The handsome young man kept asking Rose to dance, and she seemed unable to tear herself away from this stranger who danced as well as she did. During all of this time her fiancé, bursting with rage, kept eyeing Rose with a look as blazing as that of the black charger at the door. Still, it didn't deter Rose from granting the new arrival each and every dance.

At the twelve strokes of midnight the master of the house requested that everyone cease the merrymaking immediately, since it was now Ash Wednesday. Rose made a move to disengage herself but her partner held her and begged to continue, if only for a few minutes more. They were having such fun, why stop?

Of course, Rose couldn't stop, and the young couple continued to dance into Ash Wednesday while the fiddler played his infernal music as if driven by some mysterious power. Rose's little feet scarcely touched the floor. In her turnings and gyrations, she moved like a puppet—no longer subject to the laws of gravity, no longer subject to her father's dictates.

As her handsome partner drew her closer to him, he murmured in her ear that from now on she would be his, and Rose felt a painful prick in the palm of her hand. In panic she uttered a cry of despair and lost consciousness in the arms of the stranger.

Suddenly, to the astonishment of the guests, Rose's features turned ashen and her garments began to melt away, leaving her completely nude. Her handsome cavalier was also transformed. His face now looked like the mask of a demon, and with Rose in his arms he rushed out the door and made for his impatient steed.

No French Canadian legend is complete without an epic battle between Monsieur le Curé and the Devil. Every Mardi Gras, while his flock celebrated at the home of one of his parishioners, Monsieur le Curé shut himself in his study to pray for the sins his flock would undoubtedly commit. But on this Mardi Gras, while kneeling at his *priedieu*, he saw a gruesome vision. His enemy was in the act of molesting a young woman lying naked in the snow.

Aroused by the cries of the curé, the sexton dressed and rushed downstairs. As he opened the door of the study Monsieur le Curé yelled: "Isidor, quickly, go to the stable and get the grey mare."

"What has happened, Monsieur le Curé? Is someone in danger of death?"

"Worse, my son, a soul is in danger of eternal damnation. Run to the stable, there's not a moment to lose."

When the horse was ready, Monsieur le Curé galloped towards Latulippe's house. The snow was no longer falling and from a distance he could discern something stirring in front of the illuminated house. He struck the mare hard with his heels and, since she also sensed that something dreadful was about to happen, she shot forward as fast as she could. It was not a minute too soon. As the horse and rider entered the road leading to the house, another mount came towards them in a cloud of smoke and snow.

Face to face, the old enemies confronted one another above the still and naked body of the young woman, but they were unequally armed—for Monsieur le Curé had brought his stole, and he threw it over Rose's body. A cloud of fire and smoke discharged from the enemy mount, pierced by a loud, raucous cry. When the cloud had dispersed, Rose lay stretched on a square of melted snow and burnt grass. The infernal rider had disappeared.

Monsieur le Curé bent over the young girl, took off his cape, and covered her with it. After blessing her and pronouncing some Latin words, he lifted her up in his arms and carried her to the house. With his broad shoulders he brushed aside the men and women who had witnessed Rose's shameful behaviour, made his way into the living room, and gently laid his charge on the sofa. He turned towards the girl's father, threw him a long look of disapproval, and disappeared into the night without his cloak.

Of course Rose had to pay the price for her indiscretion. One version claims she became a nun, another that she remained an old maid, while another says she was married off to her fiancé and bore at least a dozen children. "There's no doubt in my mind which of these punishments is worse, but I'm not another Rose Latulippe," my mother concludes each time she tells the story.

After only two weeks on the farm in St. Bruno, it was obvious, even to a seven-year-old, that things were not going as everyone planned. The tension between my mother, my father, and my great-uncle was barely kept under control until the second Sunday, when all hell broke loose.

People had stared at us on the first Sunday we'd attended mass, but we'd assumed it was because we were strangers, new members of the congregation, or maybe because we were dressed differently from everyone else. My mother liked to dress up, and in St. Bruno, Sunday mass was the only occasion where she could wear something decent. It was an Indian summer day in late September and she wore a short-sleeved dress and a little makeup. She never overdid it—a little rouge and lipstick and a faint line of kohl on her upper eyelids. Her hair was very dark and a little colour on her face brought out the highlights, she said. She was twenty-four years old and very pretty.

I don't know how we came to sit in the first pew that Sunday but I remember everyone's eyes on us as we walked up the centre aisle, and they remained fixed on our backs throughout the first part of the mass, especially when Monsieur le Curé searched us out as he climbed the pulpit. He had the same peculiar way of speaking as everyone else in St. Bruno. The community had been isolated for so long that it had retained the accent and vocabulary of the inhabitants who had settled in the region more than two hundred years before, which explains many of the expressions my father still uses.

"God took affectionate care when he created the body of a woman from Adam's rib," Monsieur le Curé began. "He took affectionate care because he had a special role in mind for the woman's body. Her body is a receptacle, a vessel for the sacred duty of motherhood, and as we all know, my dear parishioners, each woman's body is a symbol for the vessel that carried the Son of God. There is no greater honour than that.

"There are some women, however, who believe this role is not good enough for them. Some women have the audacity to suggest, through their actions or their dress, that God didn't know his job well enough so they've decided they should help Him. They decide that in addition to being a sacred vessel for one of the most important functions of mankind, their bodies should also be adorned, painted, even exposed, because they imagine—no, my dear parishioners, they assume—that one of the body's main functions is to attract attention to itself. Yes, my dear parishioners, we have among us a Jezebel."

"I couldn't believe my ears," my mother would tell everyone in Timmins later. "I'd abandoned my home, spent the last two weeks working my fingers to the bone for a few baloney sandwiches, and here I was sitting in a dreary little church at the edge of nowhere, being called a Jezebel by some half-cocked lunatic in a cassock. I can't help it if I'm in good shape, which is hard to hide unless I wear a potato sack, but my dress didn't even have a cleavage, for god's sake. Women as vessels. Who the hell ever concocted that? You can be sure it wasn't a woman. Vassals would be more like it."

I don't suppose my mother noticed the glares, or even cared, as she stalked out in the middle of the sermon with me in tow and my father trying to keep up with us. He could stay if he wanted, she shouted when we got outside, but she and I were leaving St. Bruno on the next train. She packed our belongings and the next morning she stacked them on my uncle's wagon, the rooster chasing us out of the yard. The three of us left on the next iron horse for Timmins, my mother muttering that she was no angel but neither was she another Rose Latulippe. Clickety-clack, clickety-clack, break your grandma's back.

After the Fall Comes Winter

Tish P. Sass

The wind popped Ellen's full skirt high up on her slender legs as she stood hanging out the wash atop a grey and weathered, upside-down, wooden pop case. After she grabbed clothespins from a six-quart basket, she stuffed some into her mouth like so many cigars. Between rhythmic squeaks of the line, she pegged piece after piece of clean laundry, reaching up on tiptoes to catch flyaway corners of sheets or pillowcases. Bending and tugging wet clothes from a bushel basket, she periodically blushed almost imperceptibly when various undergarments untangled indelicately in her hands. Over and over again the choreography repeated itself.

Immense greyish clouds ran the sun-sprinkled expanse of blue high above. Nearer the horizon, billows of white and silver slid along the margins of distant hills freckled with the golds and reds of autumn. Playful waves tossed the slate green waters of the bay, while huge sky shadows spread shifting shapes over the entire landscape.

She watched the cloud of dust wind closer and closer. Suddenly she felt a sharp stirring beneath the gentle swell of her bosom.

"It's Daddy!" she murmured. Turning towards the house, she shouted, "Pop's coming home!"

Half-a-dozen eager faces swiftly assembled, grinning with anticipation. By now, they could make out the roars and rattles peculiar to Tom Farthingale's truck, cheerfully nicknamed "Old Guzzler". They laughed as one when the pickup flew over the railway tracks, its load bouncing around dangerously as the tail bumped high in the air. Soon the vehicle slammed to a halt in their laneway.

Ellen's heart burst into song at the sight of the man himself—bronzed and muscular, his curly reddish hair cropped close except across the thinning crown. His blue eyes blazed with pride over his flock as his rich voice boomed out a hearty, "Well hello there!"

The youngest children descended on him and he obligingly tickled one, patted the head of the second and scooped up a third with his powerful arms.

"My stars!" he exclaimed. "How a month's time does put the inches on you weeds...except for my darlin' Ellen that is!" Laughter rolled through him as he drew her to him and swung her around. "Yup, still light as a feather, aren't you, my gal?"

She planted a shy kiss on the stubble carpeting his face as he let her gently to the ground.

"It's good to have you home, Daddy," she breathed.

"Good to *be* home, kitten. Now where's that mother of yours? Jake, Michael—start unloadin' them cartons, will ya. We'll be celebrating Thanksgiving in style this year."

At last Hilda strode from the house, wiping flour from her thick fingers onto the apron she looped round her ample figure.

"Geez, Mother, you're lookin' good!" he pronounced, reaching forward to enfold her.

"Now Tom..." she clucked, interrupting his embrace.

"Well at least let me get a good long look at you, woman... Umm-mmh!" he smacked in approval.

Finally moved by such frank admiration, Hilda indulged him with a quick peck on his cheek. Flustered, she scolded the children back to their respective chores with a throaty, "Get cracking you! Lunch is almost ready."

"So are you glad to have me around again for a little while, Hilda honey?" Tom persisted as they strolled toward the house, adding almost as an afterthought, "I have a pretty good bundle saved for you this time what with all the hours I put in."

"Yah, but all them hours in the mines *instead* would have *kept* you home and put way more groceries on the table and clothes on our backs and maybe even..."

"Now let's not start wranglin' over that again, Hilda. You know you might as well try and cage a cardinal as get me inside the mines, and—even if you did—why it wouldn't be no time at all before that cocky redbird and me would *both* be underground—*six-feet-under* that is—and besides, a man has to..."

"Okay, OK. You can quit being so damned dramatic. After all these years I don't know why I'm expectin' miracles now anyways. C'mon—let's get to the table before you start fillin' up on some bottle!"

Sunday dawned bright, with the warmth of Indian summer embracing the gentle hills and evergreen-studded rocky cliffs.

Ellen knew she would find her father sprawled in a wicker chair on the back porch.

"Well, will ya lookee here... My. My. *My*. Why, princess, you're all dressed up! Ain't that a bit of a high heel on them shoes? Gettin' growed up fast, aren't you, kitten! But you ain't too big to sit on your daddy's knee now, are ya?"

She rushed into his outstretched arms and threw her own around his neck. After nuzzling against his chest for an instant, she freed one of her arms from the hug they held each other in.

"How's school going this year, little gal? I have me a letter or two I'd like you to pencil out when you get the time. Shouldn't be much of a problem for a high school student, now should it?"

From behind the screen door, a harsh voice suddenly cut in with, "School-school-school—that's all I ever hear from that child. And you, Tom, fillin' her silly little head with nonsense about learnin'… What good's she gonna be to any man? What good's she to any of us now most times for that matter, always wanderin' off lookin' all starry-eyed, with her nose in a book or her head in the clouds, and not carin' a fig for sewing or cooking the way my Rosie does— bless her heart. And will ya just look at that get-up she's parading around in this morning! Where'd you find that old dress, Ellen… I ain't seen it since years ago when Martha filled it out proper!"

"Now Mother—lay off the poor girl will ya? She's not hurtin' a soul, and *I* think she's purty as a picture all dolled up today." Ellen crouched into his arms, cowering against her mother's verdict as he lightly patted her arm. "Leave us be for a few minutes please, Hilda honey. We'll talk things out later, alright?"

"Hmmph!" grunted Hilda. "Later… always later. Well you just better make sure little-miss-goodie-two-shoes there gets her chores done on schedule and shows up in plenty of time to set the table at noon. It's her turn today."

He soothed his daughter with a low, "Now now now. Don't get all worked up, little princess. You mustn't pay your ma any mind when she's in one of those moods. She's gettin' near an age now where crankiness just sort of comes

natural. There there...don't take it so to heart, kitten. It ain't you who's to blame for anything. Just relax, pet."
Softly he hummed a lullaby.
The fire in the wood stove swallowed up the heat of midday. Turkey and fixin's and pumpkin pie smells teased the taste buds. Ellen slid in silently, careful to cushion the door's closing with her free hand. For a moment she stood unobserved as Hilda bustled among pots and bowls and platters.
"Mama..."
"Good Lord child!" she gasped. "You scared the wits out of me sneaking up on me like that! And you're none-too-soon getting here either! If you were any good at all you'd have already..."
"Sorry if I'm late, mama. I was getting these for you."
From behind her back Ellen extended a handful of purple splendour.
Weeds yes—but flowers foremost—and Hilda was touched by the unexpected beauty of this offering. Indulging in a rare concession toward sentiment, she softened towards her delicate offspring, in spirit with the bounty that swept the day.
"Oh, Ellen...they're lovely, child! Thank you." For a moment she absently stroked the dark wisps of hair at the girl's temples. She couldn't even explain to herself the aversion that so often coloured her relationship with a youngster whom she had to admit generally caused so little actual trouble. When compared with the boisterous antics of her others! *Different* was the only answer she could come up with, and that excuse didn't spare her a wave of guilt. If only Tom wouldn't fuss over Ellen so! It only seemed to aggravate things. And the truth was her temper needed only a surface scratch these days to set it flaring. She really must try and get hold of herself...afterall...

The sputtering of a pot-boiled-over interrupted her musings. Hailing Ellen above the sputtering and clanking, she directed, "That vase on the sill for your bouquet, girl. And since things are shaping up so fancy, let's lay the table with Grandma Fitzgerald's dishes. But be careful rooting around in that china cupboard. Now don't be a bother. I've still got work to do. Spread the tablecloth 'fore you do anything else."

Fork on the left, space for a plate, knife with the right hand, fork-space-knife, and then a round of spoons. Next came dishes from the cabinet in the living room. With concentrated caution, Ellen extricated a few at a time, admiring their pattern and gold rim as she added to her pile. *"Careful!"* she reminded herself. There. Round the table with them. *"Whew!"* she sighed. Back for the rest.

As she neared the doorway with her carefully clutched load, Ellen raised her eyes to inspect her handiwork. The silverware gleamed on the linen cloth and her vase of wild flowers enhanced the mauve in the clusters of flowers dotting the dishes.

Hilda, catching Ellen's immobility in a corner of her vision, prodded her with, "C'mon now…hurry it up!"

A thump, crash and wail shattered the next instant. In the blur that was before her, Hilda's glazed eyes focused first on the heel of a shoe caught on a scatter rug, passed over a pink rag-doll sprawled between outstretched arms, and hovered with incredulity over a seeming mountain of shards of china.

"God no!" she screamed, fury taking hold of her as the nightmare coalesced into reality. In a second the broom from the corner was in her hands. Back and forth she swept in an increasing pendulum stroke. Back and forth in a rhythm through the fragments of dishes. Back and forth right through the shimmer of sobbing taffeta. The scene quickly drew an audience of gaping mouths and rooted feet. Then Tom burst through and rushed to Ellen's side, ignoring the shouts and the blows descending on his own head. As he cradled girl towards the door, Hilda's bulk heaved against him, the broom thudding downwards from fingers now clawing ineffectually at his back.

Once outdoors he flung an arm back to free himself from his wife's hysteria and crouched near Ellen's trembling, hunched, tear-stained body.

Before he could even attempt to console her, a flurry of white squawking intervened. Stunned for a moment by disbelief he could only watch another assault on his daughter by his chicken-wielding wife. The hapless fowl was shrieking in pitiful terror, neck outstretched, wings beating uselessly against the grip the woman held its legs in. Hilda raised the hen high above her head for yet another swing at the child when Tom lunged, pinning one of his wife's hands behind her, wrenching the bird away from the other, struggling to subdue her.

Ellen bolted, running and running. The dry crunch of crumbling pale lichen, the soft spongy spring of green moss, the fuzzy brush of sumac antlers blushing red—all flowed against the staccato of clattering, clunking, grey stones loosed by her frenzied ascent. Now the summit was only a scramble away. She groped her way over a dead sapling—snapped at its base like a dry wishbone—and crawled gratefully over a bald boulder, down into a sunken hollow which had long been her private throne. In an instant the world slipped away.

One hour, then two passed. Gradually she emerged from sleep's shelter. Through her torpor, she followed the lazy drift of a bunch of bronze pine needles coasting down to a carpet of tan and orange mushrooms among dry brown ferns. Like silver spurts of flashing water, a flock of tiny

birds darted past, chirping excitedly from tree to tree and
then diving to a clump of evergreens below. One straggler
paused for a moment nearby, hanging upside down from
the tufts of a pine branch. This dapper fellow merrily
blurted out his name as he cocked a gleaming eye Ellen's
way. It seemed he might doff his black cap in greeting before
he flitted on. She smiled. Then she remembered.

She began to shiver.

Occasionally she was aware of sometimes fainter
sometimes louder echoes of her name as they searched.

The land beneath her perch lay bunched in haphazard
folds like an unwound bolt of festival paisley, its swirls of
rushing amber and vermilion punctuated by the viridian
of towering conifers. Tangled threads of lilac traced the first
denuded treetops, and fragmented beige ribbons defined
the flow of gravel roads. In a contrast of precision, the
railway cut a stark swath across the fabric, slashing the
terrain like an abandoned yardstick.

She had not registered his footsteps. When she felt the
coolness of his shadow creep over her she hid her face in
shame, convinced that not even her dear father could
forgive her what had happened.

"You'll catch your death of cold out here dressed like
that!" came the grim prediction.

It was not her father's voice.

She recognized the woodsman, whom she had often
caught glimpses of but had never talked with before.

"Here…wrap yourself up in this scarf! We'd better get
you home before it gets dark."

"I'm not *going* home."

"Nothing can be *that* bad!"

"That's what *you* think!"

"Well, little miss—if you're bound and determined not
to head home, you'd better come to my cabin for a cup of

tea to warm you up and clear your head. Maybe you'll see things differently once you've had time to think things over."

The chill of night's descent convinced her. He helped her to her feet and opened his coat, motioning her to share it with him.

As his strong arm pulled her tightly against his flank, she recognized the smell of whiskey on his breath, thought of her father, and felt comforted.

HOMEWARD

Armand Garnet Ruffo

It never failed. The telephone would ring when we least expected it, usually when the family was in the middle of something like having supper or watching television, and for a moment, as if by memory, we would all just stare at it. Myra's dark eyes would flash towards my wife Sheila, who would glance at me, take a deep breath, and finally answer it. And nearly always the same response: a moment of silence on the other end, and then click, the sound of the caller hanging up. Only occasionally would someone dare speak and actually ask for the girl. It got so we came to accept these interruptions, because we were helpless to do anything about them even though everyone knew that contact was supposed to be both minimal and regulated. Sheila had spoken to Myra's child welfare worker until she was blue in the face, and it seemed to do no good whatsoever. "I'll speak to them" was the rehearsed response. And still the calls came from her mother and father at all hours and more often than not when they were more than a little high.

What we didn't realize is that the parents were not only after the girl but also her brothers and sisters. We knew that she was seeing them regularly, if not at school, then around town, but we didn't know that her parents—and we should have realized it—were also trying to get at Myra through her brothers and sisters. They had a planted a seed that had taken root in the other kids, and it was now winding its way into Myra: one day they would all live together as one big happy family. The families they were now living with did not really love them and had taken them in only for the money. They should never forget that they were supposed to do whatever they could to join their real parents in Sudbury. Did I mention they were all going to live happily-ever-after?

And so feeling the ache of abandonment, she went to her case worker at the Children's Aid Society and asked to be moved back to her parents. Only twelve and here she was making her own decisions about where she wanted to live. CAS, which had legal custody over her, never once thought that a move might not be in her best interest. When she finally told us we were both heartbroken and worried for her. We could tell that the decision to go was also tearing her apart, because despite what her parents had planted inside her, she had also become part of our family. We had come to think of her as our own daughter. She had been living with us in our home on the reserve for three years, but I guess we knew this day was coming. They had been constantly at her—she had never really been given a chance to make a new start for herself. Nevertheless, we sat her down at the kitchen table and had a long talk. We told her that sometimes what we imagine might not be reality. We asked her to think hard about her decision and try to remember what it had been like living with them. We reminded her that she had come to us because they had been having problems, and from all accounts, they were still having the same problems. But she had made up her mind and nothing we could say or do could change it.

"Are you sure?"

"I have to."

"You don't have to do anything you don't want to."

"I want to."

"Well we'd like to say you can't go, but we can't. You know that don't you?"

In the end, our conversation led to a dead-end, with her staring at the floor and nodding her head, and all we could do was wipe our eyes and give her a warm hug. We never specifically mentioned her parents' cocaine addiction or the alcohol, and maybe we should have, but we hoped they were over it, and we also knew that somewhere beyond all the crap, they loved her and she loved them. And maybe that was enough. We did tell her that they still might not be ready for her, that she should be prepared. Looking back though, maybe we should have been harsher and told her the blunt facts, but that is not our way, and, besides, if a strong-willed kid like Myra wanted to be with her parents, little or nothing anybody said or did could stop her once her mind was made up. It was her decision to make, and she chose to leave us.

I can still see the ragged nine year old being dropped off at our place that first day, meeting the other children who had come to live with us from other reserves and lives as chaotic as her own. I think she was surprised to see such a difference between the way we lived and where she had come from, constantly bounced around with her brothers and sisters, waking up surrounded by a party of strangers. Living beside the calm of Fox Lake proved to be a blessing for her because she loved to fish and would spend hours out on the water. Or she would come with me when I went out to some of the distant lakes in the region and did what I called some serious fishing. When I asked the kids if anyone would like to come along, she was always the first to jump up and would already have her boots on before any of the others even made a move. The same with hunting. Because tracking moose is mostly about keeping still, the other kids usually lost interest pretty quickly, and generally preferred to stay at home. Not Myra. Again, she would have her boots and coat on and would be sitting in the cab of the truck before I even got my gear together. What she didn't like was school. And I think this had more to do with having to deal with teachers and other children than the actual schoolwork. Everybody in town knew who her birth family was, that her sisters and brothers were also in foster care, that her parents' names had shown up in the newspaper, and I think the town kids especially gave her a hard time about it. If it bothered her, she didn't acknowledge it. What was obvious though is that aside from her family, she had no friends. Except one, and an odd one it was—my own father.

After my mother died and I married Sheila, I began having him over for Sunday supper. Seeing that he was living alone, I figured he could use the company. He seemed to enjoy having the kids around and soon became their grumpy grandpa. I say grumpy because of his perpetual negative attitude towards what he called modern life, and because he normally didn't say much—which is perhaps why he hit it off with Myra, who also had to be squeezed to get two words out of her. While he was pleasant enough, after supper he always found some excuse to leave. Whether it was to feed the cat or walk the dog, there was always something. At first he would force himself to sit with the family, but his unease became obvious, which led to a stilted formality, and it was soon apparent that it was better for everyone to let him go. But the old man was changing, because he could now be seen gabbing with other scruffy old-timers like himself, standing in front of the post office or sitting on a stool in Stedman's over coffee. What I came to realize was that his so-called gabbing was something he did simply to kill time. For him, old age had taken away everything he had known. With his wife gone and without the ability to get around like he used to, get out in the bush for weeks on end to hunt and fish, disappear in his own independence, life had become a series of nights watching television and days riding around alone in his old blue Rambler, checking the bush roads for signs of animal life. Until Myra showed up, that is.

Since she had no use for school, her education became a pattern of leaving at lunchtime and heading over to my father's house to join him in his daily travels. Of course this was something I only heard about later when Sheila happened to find one of the many notes from her teacher that Myra was supposed to give us. Why the teacher never pursued the matter when we didn't respond to her request for a meeting, I can only assume had to do with us living on a reserve and the fact that nothing much was expected of Native kids anyway. As for my father, he was the last person in the world to give two hoots if Myra went to school or not. This is not to say that he didn't see value in education, and he certainly never prevented my sister or me from going to school, but he believed that in some cases it could do more harm than good. He liked to quote the old axiom that a little learning is a dangerous thing, and as a case in point he referred to the politicians running the country.

Although my father was white himself, most folks who met him commented that he should have been born an Indian, or at least a voyageur, a couple hundred years ago. As for my mother, who indeed was Indian, Ojibway to be exact, she loved the bush as much as he did, and this they shared intimately. She nevertheless deserved a medal for putting up with him for forty years. Running water and electricity did not have to be forced upon her, but if the town hadn't made everyone hook up to the grid, my father would no doubt still be cooking on a woodstove and lighting his house with kerosene lamps, which I might add complemented his flannel shirts, long underwear and buck knife strapped to his belt. I use the word "house" here loosely because with its rotten foundation and leaky flat roof, and its assortment of windows salvaged from the dump, it was really little more than a shack. And when the town itself experienced a small boom due to the rising price of lumber, its main industry, and new houses were going up all around him, my father was perfectly oblivious to it all. No matter what I or my mother or anybody said, he ignored us all. Why worry about something as mundane as a leaky roof when you could be reeling in a pickerel and soaking up the tranquility of a lakeshore supper. Though once in a while he did complain that his own little patch of what used to be the edge of town was becoming increasingly crowded. It goes without saying that when the town council tried to buy his lot from him to demolish the eyesore, he wouldn't hear of it. And as for his new flush toilet, the town had to force it on him by giving him notice to get rid of the outhouse or else. They tried to be delicate about it, but it was a bit of an anomaly to see a shack and outhouse in the middle of a new housing development.

In their own quiet way, Myra and my father became companions of the trail, best buddies even. Myra would show up for lunch, and my father would have his special soup on. Because of a heart condition, he had been told to stop eating fried food. Taking the doctor at his word, he literally threw his fry pan out the window, from then on mostly boiling or barbequing everything, except for what we liked to call *the soup*. No one else would go near it let alone eat it except Myra. There was no recipe and the ingredients changed depending on what he had in the cupboards and refrigerator. The basis for the soup was always the same: a package of chicken noodle soup. From there he added whatever was on hand, the variations including moosemeat, ground beef, ham, ribs, potatoes, rice, eggs, onions, celery, tomatoes, carrots…with a good dash of salt and pepper. He and Myra would gobble up the concoction with toast and tea and then head out to one of the old logging roads to check on the animals. To this day, I can't imagine what they talked about, this odd old man and the solitary girl, but it surely must have had something to do with the birds and the beaver, the fox and the moose they might have encountered that day. Although it sounds cliché, I have to say that my father knew the bush like the back of his hand, like a farmer knows his fields, a gardener his garden, and he could not have found a better pupil than Myra.

And still it was not enough to keep her with us. I wonder if I had asked him to try to get her to stay, would it have made a difference. But it didn't occur to me at the time because we figured that Myra knew we were all going to miss her, and, like I said, she had already made up her mind. Besides, a couple of months earlier, one of my father's friends, widowed like himself, had accused Myra of stealing money from her. She had come to visit my father one afternoon at lunchtime when Myra happened to be there and had left her purse on a kitchen chair while she and my father went outside to look at my mother's garden. (After Mom died he had let her flower garden go to hell.) Myra had stayed inside stirring the infamous soup. When Mrs. Labelle later checked her purse she was supposedly missing five dollars. Myra swore to us that she never touched the purse, and, frankly, I believed her. I thought the old lady probably just imagined she had an extra five dollars. Sheila thought she did it on purpose, because she was jealous of my father's affection for Myra. As for my father, he didn't know what to think and had no problem paying back the money, but I sensed his bond with Myra was strained after that. Anyway, I didn't involve my father in Myra's decision to leave. I simply told him, and he came over to say goodbye. He drove his Rambler into the yard, honked a couple times, and got out and stood by the car. Myra went out to meet him. I don't know what they said, but I saw them hug, and then without even coming in, the old man drove away. And that was it.

And that was the last time any of us saw her. Everything we feared came true. Just today I learned in a call from her grandparents that nothing had changed with Myra's parents, that she should never have gone back to them. Of course, her parents welcomed all their kids with open arms, and were only too willing to share their problems with them. One of Myra's brothers, only a year older, was already hooked on crack cocaine. There were no rules for the kids; they came and went as they pleased, ate and drank as they pleased, did anything they wanted. I suspect that Myra too got caught up in this lifestyle because we didn't hear from her for about a year. And then we got a call that she wanted to come home—to our home. I told her to stay put, and I would make arrangements to come and get her, but she said she had a ride. Determined to get back to us as quickly as possible, she ended up stealing a car. Not yet fourteen years old, and here she was trying to drive at night all the way from Sudbury, a distance of over 400 kilometers on mostly deserted winding highway. Barely able to see over the dashboard, with too much speed, she lost control of the car going around a sharp curve just north of Cartier. We were told the car ended up crushed in a rock-cut like a tin can.

Home. That dream of being surrounded by the people you love in a place you can call your own, a place where you belong. We had tried our utmost to give her this, and yet, in the end we failed, because we could not become what she wanted most of all: her family. She would not let us. They too would not let us and never once let her forget it. Where do we go from here? I will never look at the children we have given shelter to in the same way again. Because of what happened to Myra, I now realize more than ever the turmoil that these kids live through. The past is always alive pumping inside us, and it is often marked with deep gashes that never heal or fade, especially when in the form of a distant voice pleading with you to come home. The voice you first heard rocking you to sleep in your cradle. How could we be heard over that? Our voice resided in the present, and it was muffled and lost to the past that became her life. The little girl who could spend days without saying a word and then suddenly break into laughter at seeing two squirrels chasing each other in circles. If only the laughter had been enough.

My wife is in the other room with the children. They are all crying. I am trying to focus on tying the laces of my boots, but I keep fumbling with them because I can't help keep thinking of the terror that must have been on Myra's face as she tried to keep the car on the road and knew she was losing it. Her hands gripped to the steering wheel, her leg extended as she strained for the brake and probably couldn't reach it. And then the wall of rock. I keep thinking of this as I finally get my boots tied, put on my coat, and go out the door. When I get to my truck I can't even bring myself to start it but just sit in the cab and bang the steering wheel. Why a car? Why not money to buy a bus or train ticket? I turn on the ignition, then the headlights, and pull out of the yard onto the darkened road. When I'm almost off the rez a fox crosses my path; its yellow eyes flash at me, a signal that life is still going on all around me even in the pitch of this dark night.

I know the old man will already be in bed by the time I get over to his place, but this news can't wait until morning. It's also something I can't tell him over the telephone, though I'm not sure why. When my mother was alive she acted as our intermediary. Nearly everything we wanted to ask each other went through her. We never seemed to be able to find the words to express what we really wanted to say. With her passing, the silence between us widened into a chasm. Yet, more than ever I need to see him and tell him what happened face to face. I'm not sure what he'll say. Maybe he will blame me for letting her go. Maybe he will blame her parents and curse them. Maybe he will cry like the others. Maybe we will hug. If we do, it will be the first time for both of us. Maybe this time he will not close the door and turn away alone.

HEARTS AND FLOWERS

Tomson Highway

Daniel Daylight sits inside Mr. Tipper's travelling car. It is cold—not cold, though, like outside; of this fact Daniel Daylight is quite certain. He looks out through the window on his right and, as always, sees white forest rushing by; maybe rabbits will bound past on that snowbank in the trees, he sits thinking. He has seen them, after all, on past Thursdays just like this one. It is dark, too. Not pitch-black, though, for that half moon hangs unhidden, making snow—on the road, on the roadside, rocks, ground, trees (mostly spruce though some birch and some poplar)—glow, as with dust made of silver, Daniel Daylight sits there thinking. Daniel Daylight, at age eight, is on his way to his piano lesson in Prince William, Manitoba.

Twenty miles lie between the Watson Lake Indian Residential School, where resides Daniel Daylight, and Prince William, where he takes his weekly lesson. The Watson Lake Indian Residential School, after all, has no one to teach him how to play the piano, while Prince William has elderly and kind Mrs. Hay. So his teacher in Grade Three at the Watson Lake Indian Residential School, Mr. Tipper, drives him every Thursday, 6:00 p.m. on the nose, to his piano teacher's house, Mrs. Hay's, in Prince William.

Orange brick and cement from the top to the bottom, held in by a steel mesh fence, then by forest (mostly spruce though some birch and some poplar), the Watson Lake Indian Residential School stands like a fort on the south shore of a lake called Watson Lake, 550 miles north of Winnipeg, Mr. Tipper's place of birth. Prince William, quite by contrast, is a town that stands on the south bank of a river called the Moostoos River, just across from which sprawls a village called Waskeechoos (though "settlement" is a noun more accurate, Mr. Tipper has explained on previous Thursdays, for no "village" can be seen, only houses peeking out of the forest here and there). Waskeechoos, on the north bank of the muddy Moostoos River, is an Indian reserve, Mr. Tipper has informed Daniel Daylight, not unlike the one from which hails Daniel Daylight: Minstik Lake, Manitoba, 350 miles north of Waskeechoos, Prince William, and the Watson Lake Indian Residential School. It takes half an hour for Daniel Daylight to make the journey every week, in Mr. Tipper's travelling car, from the Watson Lake Indian Residential School south through the heart of Waskeechoos and across the Moostoos River to Prince William, so he has time on his hands for reflection (so, at least, Mr. Tipper calls such thinking).

Daniel Daylight likes these trips. For one thing, he gets to practise what he knows of the language they call English with elderly and kind Mrs. Hay, with the waiters at the Nip House or at Wong's (where he sometimes goes for snacks with Mr. Tipper once he's finished with his lesson), and with friends of Mr. Tipper whom he meets at the Nip House or at Wong's. He enjoys speaking English just as he enjoys speaking Cree with the students at the residential school (though, of course, mother tongues need no practice, not like English with its *v*'s that make one's teeth come right out and bite one's lower lip). Daniel Daylight, for another thing, likes to ride in "travelling cars" (as he calls them for the *v* in "travel"). Standing at the northern tip of a lake called Minstik Lake, the Minstik Lake Indian Reserve, after all, has no cars and no trucks, just dogsleds in the winter, canoes in the summer. A third reason why Daniel Daylight likes these trips is that he enjoys being dazzled by the lights of a city like Prince William (for to him, the railway depot is a city of one million, not a town of five thousand) with its streets, its cafés, hotels, stores, and huge churches with tall steeples, whereas Minstik Lake, with its six hundred people, has no streets, no cafés, no hotels, just dirt paths, one small store, and one church. Daniel Daylight, for a fourth thing, likes these trips because Mr. Tipper's travelling car has a radio that plays songs that he can learn in his head. When it stops playing music, furthermore, it plays *spoken* English words, which, of course, he can practise understanding. Tonight, for example, people living in the east of the country (Mr. Tipper has explained) are discussing voting patterns of the nation (Mr. Tipper has explained), even though Daniel Daylight knows the word "vote" for one reason: it begins with the sound that forces one to sink one's teeth deep into one's lower lip and then growl. Sound, that is to say, thrills Daniel Daylight. Which is why, best of all, Daniel Daylight likes these trips: because he gets to play the piano. He gets to play, for elderly and kind Mrs. Hay, "Sonatina" by Clementi, which he now knows well enough to play page 1 from the top to the bottom without stopping. He gets to play, for the third time this winter, "Pirates of the Pacific," with the bass that sounds like a drumbeat. He gets to play, this week, for the first time, *with* Jenny Dean, the duet—for four hands—called "Hearts and Flowers."

"Jenny Dean is a white girl," he has overheard someone

say at the Nip House, just a few days before Christmas, in fact, when he was there having fries and Coca-Cola with Mr. Tipper. "Daniel Daylight is an *Indian*. A Cree Indian. Indian boys do *not* play the piano with white girls," he has overheard one white girl whisper *loudly* to another over Coca-Cola in a bottle, "not here in our Prince William, not anywhere on earth or in heaven." Daniel Daylight let it pass. He, after all, was eight years old, not thirty-one like Mr. Tipper; what could he have done to the girl who had made such a statement? Bop her on the head with her bottle? Shove a french fry up her nose? Scratch her face? Besides, neither Jenny Dean's parents, Mrs. Hay, nor Mr. Tipper seemed to mind the notion of Jenny Dean making music with a boy whose father was a *Cree* caribou hunter and a celebrated dogsled racer.

"There it is," says Mr. Tipper. And so it is, for the travelling car has just rounded the bend in the road from which the lights of Prince William and the Indian reserve on this side of the river from the town can be seen for the first time. This first view of both town and reserve, to Daniel Daylight, always looks like a spaceship landed on Planet Earth, not unlike the spaceship in the comic book that his older brother, John-Peter Daylight, gave him as a Christmas present twenty-one days ago and that Daniel Daylight keeps hidden under his pillow in the dormitory at the residential school. Daniel Daylight likes, in fact, to imagine all those lights in the distance as exactly that: a spaceship come to take him to a place where exist not Indian people, not white people, just good people and good music. In fact, he can hear in his mind already "Sonatina" by Clementi, key of G, allegro moderato. He can hear "Pirates of the Pacific" with that drumbeat in the bass that goes *boom*. He can hear "Hearts and Flowers." He has practised all three pieces to the point of exhaustion, after all, in the one room at the residential school that has a piano, what the nuns and the priests call the "library" but, in fact, is a storage room for pencils and erasers, papers, rulers, chalk, and some old spelling books. Feeling on the tips of his fingers all the keys of Mrs. Hay's brown piano, Daniel Daylight sees the sign on the roadside that announces, "Waskeechoos Welcomes You." Mr. Tipper's travelling car speeds past the sign, thus bringing Daniel Daylight onto land that belongs "to the Indians," Mr. Tipper, for some reason, likes proclaiming, as on a radio. "Speed Limit 30 mph," Daniel Daylight reads on the sign that then follows. The road now mud, dried, cracked, and frozen, pot-holed and iced, the travelling car first slows down to a crawl, then bumps, rattles, slides.

"Indian people are not human," says Mr. Tipper, dodging first this small patch of ice then that small patch of ice, "at least not according to the government. They cannot vote." Daniel Daylight sits unsurprised—Mr. Tipper's use of English, white as a sheet and from Winnipeg as he may be, is not always perfect, Daniel Daylight has simply come to accept. The young Cree piano player, in any case, does not feel confident enough, in either his grasp of English *or* his age, to say much in rebuttal. His father, after all, speaks maybe ten words of English, his mother just two or three; of his eight living siblings, older all than him, only John-Peter Daylight, who is three grades ahead of Daniel Daylight at the Watson Lake Indian Residential School (and perhaps Florence, who once studied there, too, but quit at just Grade Four), speaks English. No one on the Minstik Lake Indian Reserve where Daniel Daylight was born, for that matter, speaks the language, not even Chief Samba Cheese Weetigo or his wife, Salad. Like people right here in Waskeechoos (as Mr. Tipper has informed Daniel Daylight in the past), they speak Cree and Cree only. So how, indeed, *can* they be human, Daniel Daylight asks himself, *if* they don't even know what the word means or looks like on a page?

At the bridge that spans like a giant spider's web the muddy, winding Moostoos River, a bottleneck is fast taking shape. Built mainly for trains, the bridge makes room for car and truck traffic only by means of a one-way lane off to one side. The traffic light glowing red like a charcoal on this side of the crossing, four cars sit at its base humming and putt-putt-putting; the travellers from Watson, as happened last Thursday, will just have to sit there for four or five minutes, much too long for Daniel Daylight, who can't wait to play the piano with Jenny Dean. Preparing, in a sense, for conversing with elderly and kind Mrs. Hay when he gets to her house (for Mrs. Hay's Cree, of course, is like Mr. Tipper's—it does not exist), Daniel Daylight makes a decision: he will practise his English. On Mr. Tipper.

"Human, what it mean, Mr. Tip—" But Mr. Tipper does not let him finish.

"If a man, or a woman, aged twenty-one or older cannot vote," says Mr. Tipper—who, from the side, resembles Elmer Fudd, Bugs Bunny's worst enemy in the comics, thinks Daniel Daylight—"then how on earth can he be human, hmmm, Daniel Daylight?"

"'Vote'?" Daniel Daylight feels himself bite his thick lower lip with both sets of teeth, so unlike Cree which has no such sound or letter, he sits there regretting.

"'Vote' is when a person helps choose the leaders that will make the laws for his country," replies Mr. Tipper. He snorts once and then continues. "Every four years, in Winnipeg where I come from, for instance, the person who has the right to vote will go to a church or a school or some such building that has a hall, step inside a little...room—

the *voting* booth, this room is called—take a small piece of paper on which are written the names of the four, five, or six people from that region or that neighbourhood who want to go to Ottawa to speak for the people of that region or that neighbourhood." Daniel Daylight is having trouble keeping up with the torrent of words pouring out of Mr. Tipper's mouth. Still, he manages to catch what he thinks Mr. Tipper, in the past, has referred to as "the drift." "The person then votes—that is to say, chooses—by checking off the name of the person on that list who he thinks will best speak for him and his needs, and the person on that list whose name ends up being checked off by the greatest number of people in that region or that neighbourhood is voted, in this way, into power, and that person goes to Ottawa to help our prime minister run our country, is what the word 'vote' means, Daniel Daylight," says Mr. Tipper. "You 'vote' for your leader. *You* decide how *you* want *your* life to be in *your* country. That's what makes you a human. Otherwise, you're not."

The traffic light changes first to yellow, then to green. Daniel Daylight has always taken pleasure in looking at what, to him, is an act of magic. *Thump*, *thump*, goes the travelling car as it crosses the bridge built for trains. The *thump*, *thump* stops. And now they're in Prince William (or in land that is human, as Mr. Tipper calls it, where people can "vote," just like in Winnipeg)—paved streets, lights so bright Daniel Daylight has to squint, lights so bright it looks like mid-afternoon. On Mr. Tipper's car radio, the music is back; some sad, lonely man is howling away about being "cheated" by someone, maybe his wife. To Daniel Daylight, it sounds, for some reason, like the Indians are being cheated.

In Mrs. Hay's living room, Daniel Daylight sits straight-backed at her upright Baldwin piano. Sitting in a chair right beside him, her hairdo white, short, and fluffy, her face as wrinkled as prunes, the elderly and kind human woman smiles at her one Cree student through glasses so thick they could be ashtrays, Daniel Daylight sits there thinking. Scales first, chords next, then arpeggios, key of E. Major. Right hand only, two octaves up: E, G-sharp, B, E, G-sharp, B, E. And two octaves down: E, G-sharp, B, E, G-sharp, B, E. Back up, back down, Mrs. Hay humming softly along, in her cracked, quavery voice, with the tune such as it is. Daniel Daylight cannot help but wonder as he plays his arpeggio in E major if playing the piano will or will not make him human. Left hand next, same arpeggio, only two octaves lower, first up: E, G-sharp, B, E, G-sharp, B, E. And two octaves down: E, G-sharp, B, E, G-sharp, B, E. He is dying to stop right there at the E with the brown stain and confront Mrs. Hay with the question, for Mr. Tipper, as always, has left him with her, alone, at her house for the hour.

"Very good, Danny," says Mrs. Hay, giving him no chance to ask any questions. Only she, of all the people he knows in the world, calls or has called him Danny. Not his five older brothers, not his six older sisters, not his one hundred friends, not even his parents call him "Danny Daylight." Daniel Daylight is not sure he likes it. But he says nothing. In any case, it's too late now; she has called him "Danny" ever since he first walked into her house that fine, sunny day in September almost three years ago. They move on. First "Sonatina" by Clementi, key of G, allegro moderato, a Grade Six piece; of this fact, Daniel Daylight is very proud if only because he has been taking piano lessons for only two and a half years and should, by rights, still be in Grade Three, not Grade Six already.

"It's the 14th of January," says Mrs. Hay as she peers

over her glasses at the calendar that hangs on the wall with
the picture, right above the calendar's big, black "1960," of
her husband, Mr. Hay, driving a train and smiling and
waving. "The festival starts on the 29th of March." Daniel
Daylight thus has ten weeks to practise and memorize
"Sonatina," for that is his solo entry at the festival and he
plans nothing less than to win first prize. As he plays
"Sonatina," a piece energetic and happy because it, after
all, is written in the key of G, major, allegro moderato
(meaning, in Italian, "fast, but not too fast," as in
"moderate"), Daniel Daylight, in his mind, sees his father,
Cheechup Daylight, and his mother, Adelaide, standing in
a line at the little wooden church in the village of Minstik
Lake, a worn yellow pencil each in hand. They are lining
up to vote. At this point in their lives, they are not human,
for a sign on their backs says as much: "Non- human." The
melody line for Clementi's "Sonatina" soars like a swallow
flying up to the clouds, tugging at the heart of Daniel
Daylight as with a rope. If he plays it well enough, his
parents will surely turn, allegro moderato, into humans,
Daniel Daylight prays as he plays. He comes to the end:
dominant chord (his right thumb adding the minor seventh)
followed, *seemak* (right away), by the tonic. *Thump. Thump.*
In the pianist's mind, Cheechup Daylight and his wife,
Adelaide, are turned away from the little voting booth by
the missionary priest, Father Roy. They are not human. They
cannot vote.

"Very good, Danny," says Mrs. Hay. "Jenny should be
here in just five minutes," she adds, smiling. "But..." And
this is where Mrs. Hay, kind as a *koogoom* (grandmother)
as she may be, criticizes him and his playing, sometimes in
a manner that takes him quite by surprise. He is tensing up
at his right temple as he plays, says Mrs. Hay. If he is tensing
up, at his right temple, meaning to say that a vein pops up

in that region, as she calls it, every time he reaches for a high note, then his right arm is tensing up and if his right arm is tensing up then his right hand is tensing up. Which is why the melody, from measure 17 to measure 21, in particular, sounds not very happy, forced, not quite "there," explains Mrs. Hay. He must try it again. He does, Mrs. Hay, this time, holding her bone-thin, liver-spotted, white right hand, gentle as a puff of absorbent cotton, on Daniel Daylight's thin right wrist, guiding him, as it were, from phrase to phrase to phrase. Better this time, he can feel it: his right arm is not tensing up, not as much anyway. Again, however, as "Sonatina" comes to an end, his parents are turned away from the little cardboard booth at the church that stands on the hill overlooking the northern extremity of Minstik Lake. *Still*, they are not human. *Ding*, goes Mrs. Hay's electric doorbell. And into the vestibule of her back entrance blow a flurry of snow *and* Jenny Dean. Taking off her bulky winter outerwear—mitts, coat, hat, scarf, boots— her cheeks glow pink from the cold of a mid-January evening in far north Manitoba and her hazel cat-like eyes sparkle as does her blond, curly hair—yes, decides Daniel Daylight, Jenny Dean looks, indeed, like a human.

Now Jenny Dean is sitting on the brown wooden bench right there beside Daniel Daylight. She smells so nice, thinks Daniel Daylight, like snow just fallen on a green spruce bough. The sheet music for the duet Mrs. Hay has chosen as their entry at the festival sits open on the piano's music stand before them. He can feel his red-flannel-sleeved right arm pressing up against the girl's yellow-pullovered left arm. His is the lower part, the part with the bass line and chord structure, hers the higher part, the part with the melody but with the occasional *part* of a chord, meaning that the Cree Indian, non-human pianist, the "Heart," Daniel Daylight, and the white girl human pianist, the

"Flower," Jenny Dean, will be sharing chords, in public, from a piece of music called "Hearts and Flowers" written in the key of C, major, andante cantabile—meaning, in Italian, "at a walking pace *and* singing"—by a human woman named Joan C. McCumber.

Water-like, limpid, and calm, the chords start playing, they float, placed with care on the keyboard by Daniel Daylight. The bass sneaks in, the melody begins. Playing octaves, Jenny Dean's hands begin at the two Cs above middle C, arc up to the G in a curve graceful and smooth, then waft back down to the F, move on down to the E, and thence to the D, skip down to the B and swerve back up to the C whence they had started. The melody pauses, Daniel Daylight's series of major chords billow out to fill the silence, the melody resumes with another arcing phrase, filled with sunlight. For Daniel Daylight, two things happen. First, from where he sits, he sees four hands, two brown (non-human), two white (human), playing the piano. He is sure, somehow, that once he and Jenny Dean have mastered the piece and won first prize in the duet section of the music festival, he—and his parents—will be human. They will have the vote. Father Roy will *not* be able to turn Cheechup Daylight and his wife, Adelaide, away from the little voting booth at the little wooden church that overlooks the northern extremity of beautiful, extraordinary Minstik Lake with its ten thousand islands.

One month later, Daniel Daylight sits at a table in a booth at the Nip House on Prince William's main thoroughfare, looking with amazement at the valentine just given him, at Mrs. Hay's, by the human piano player Jenny Dean. Standing upright on the table one foot before him, the card is covered with hearts and flowers. High above it looms the very white face of Mr. Tipper with his

Elmer-Fudd-like, round, pudgy nose, and behind Mr. Tipper, a wall made of one giant mirror. On the radio that sits on the counter five tables, and therefore five booths, behind Daniel Daylight, Kitty Wells is singing, "Three Ways to Love You, It's True," his sister, Florence Daylight's, favourite song, the one she sings with her boyfriend, Alec Cook, as they sit there on the shores of Minstik Lake strumming and strumming their two old guitars. Now it is mid-February, the Kiwanis Music Festival looms even closer—just six weeks, Mrs. Hay has informed Daniel Daylight and Jenny Dean, so Daniel Daylight is excited to the point where he can't stop slurping, through a straw and as loudly as he can, at his glass half-filled with black Coca-Cola. They are sitting in the "Indians Only" section of the restaurant, Mr. Tipper, for some reason, chooses this moment to explain to Daniel Daylight, his blue eyes peering at the restaurant spread out behind and over Daniel Daylight's shoulder. Daniel Daylight stops his slurping and peers past the rim of the tall thin glass at the wall behind Mr. Tipper, the wall which, of course, is one giant mirror. Darting his eyeballs about like tiny searchlights, he looks for a sign that will, indeed, say "Indians Only."

"There is no sign that says 'Indians only,'" says Mr. Tipper, knowing, as almost always, what is going on inside the mind of Daniel Daylight.

"Indians only..." Kitty Wells has stopped singing, Daniel Daylight suddenly observes, and a man's speaking voice has taken over on the radio. Daniel Daylight locks his eyes with Mr. Tipper's—what on earth will the man say next about...?

"Hamburger deluxe, gravy on the side!" yells the big, fat waitress who always scowls at Daniel Daylight, drowning out the voice of the man on the radio, at least temporarily.

"...cannot vote," the man on the radio ends his speech. "You see?" says Mr. Tipper, sipping at his coffee with his thick purplish lips. "They're not human, not according to the radio, not according to the government. It is the law."

"Who made the law?" Daniel Daylight feels emboldened to ask Mr. Tipper.

"No one," says Mr. Tipper. "They are unwritten. It's the same thing at the movie house right here in Prince William, the taverns, the bingo hall, even the churches, Baptist, Anglican, *and* Catholic—Indians on one side, whites on the other."

Suddenly ignoring his half-finished plate of french fries with gravy, his Coke, and his valentine, Daniel Daylight twists his back around to look at the rest of the restaurant—looking in the mirror will *not* do: 1) the Nip House has room for at least sixty customers; 2) the fire-engine-red-vinyl-covered booths are not high enough to hide anyone from anyone; 3) true to Mr. Tipper's unwanted observation, white people sit on one side of the restaurant, Indian people on the other. He turns back to the mirror and to Mr. Tipper, who, of course, is the one exception, being as he is a white man sitting with the brown-skinned, black-haired, non-human, Cree Indian pianist Daniel Daylight on the "Indians Only" side of the restaurant. Mr. Tipper must be brave, Daniel Daylight thinks rather sadly, lets go his Coke, and slips his valentine into a pocket of his black woollen parka. Suddenly, he is no longer hungry.

Six weeks later, Daniel Daylight sits inside Mr. Tipper's travelling car with the radio playing, again, country music, a song that Daniel Daylight does not know. He is about to ask when Mr. Tipper asks him, "What will they think when they see you and Jenny Dean playing together at the festival?" Daniel Daylight has no answer, not at the moment anyway, for "They will love our music" sounds somehow hypocritical, facetious, not quite truthful. Again they are going down the winding gravel road, with snow-covered forest rushing by as always, a rabbit bounding past on the snowbank just to the right. Daniel Daylight is on his way, this time, to the Kiwanis Music Festival in Prince William. He is going there to compete in the solo/Grade Six section with his "Sonatina" by Clementi, key of G, allegro moderato, which he now has down note-perfect *and* memorized. More important, however—at least so says Mr. Tipper, and with this notion Daniel Daylight is inclined to agree—he is going there to compete in the duet section of the annual event with the white girl/human, Jenny Dean, in a piece with the title "Hearts and Flowers," written by the human composer Joan C. McCumber.

They come to the Indian reserve called Waskeechoos, the sign that says so just going by and the next one saying "Speed Limit 30 mph." The travelling car slows down. It bumps, rocks, and rattles. One pot-hole here, two there. Ice. The travelling car slides once, for six inches, then stops. A non-human man walks past, from the town and back to his home in Waskeechoos.

"People can't vote?" asks Daniel Daylight, his English, and his confidence, having bloomed rather nicely in the last two months for, of course, it is now the 31st of March, 1960, the last day of the three-day-long Kiwanis Music Festival, and northern Manitoba is still gripped hard by winter.

"Soon they might," says Mr. Tipper. "I heard on the radio the other day..." But the traffic light at the railway bridge has just turned green and Daniel Daylight, in any case, has drifted off already to his own reserve 350 miles north, where his father and his mother are standing in line at the church on the hill that overlooks beautiful, extraordinary Minstik Lake, a worn yellow pencil each in hand. They are getting ready to select a man they can send to Ottawa to speak for Minstik Lake and all its people, perhaps even Chief Samba Cheese Weetigo. Into the line behind and in front of them are crushed all six hundred people of Minstik Lake, even babies. And they are roaring; they want to vote. "Apparently the law is changing," says Mr. Tipper, "soon. Or so I heard on the radio." Good, thinks Daniel Daylight, all these people back there in Waskeechoos, like those people where I come from, will soon be human, he sits there thinking. He doesn't even notice that they are now on "human territory," as Mr. Tipper calls it, for already he can see himself on stage at the Kiwanis Auditorium in downtown Prince William, sitting at the piano beside Jenny Dean, playing music with all his might so his parents, and therefore he, can change from non-human to human. He is glad that Sister St. Alphonse, the principal seamstress at the Watson Lake Indian Residential School, has found him a suit for the evening: black, white shirt, red necktie, black shoes, all, for the moment, under his black woollen parka. His hands, meanwhile, are wrapped in woollen mittens so thick they do *not* stand a chance of getting cold, stiff, or claw-like, he has decided, not when he has to use them, tonight, to make a *point*.

At the Kiwanis Auditorium in downtown Prince William, Daniel Daylight sits in the audience with his back tall and straight, like all good pianists, Mrs. Hay has always insisted. From where he sits, in the middle and on the room's right side, he can see—now that he is two months wiser, courtesy of Mr. Tipper—that the room is, indeed, divided: white people on one side, Indian people on the other, the latter a little on the sparse side. Just like at the

Nip House and at Wong's, Daniel Daylight sits there and thinks, *and* at the movies, the bingo hall, the taverns, and the churches—according, anyway, to Mr. Tipper, who has been to all these places. As he sits there waiting for his turn on stage, he can, on the left side of the hall, see Jenny Dean and her parents, with Mrs. Hay, waving at him and waving at him, beckoning him to come to their side. Shyly, he shakes his head. Jenny Dean, with her parents, belongs on the human side, he, with his parents (who are not only non-human but absent) on the other. Only Mr. Tipper sits beside him, and he is not even supposed to be there. On stage, some dreadful music is playing: two human boys at the piano, aged ten years or so (guesses Daniel Daylight), wearing green V-neck sweaters, white shirts, and bowties, their hair yellow as hay, skin white as cake mix. According to the program, they are playing a duet called "Squadrons of the Air" but Daniel Daylight can't really tell; whatever the word "squadrons" means, it sounds like they are dropping bombs from the air on some poor hapless village. Next come two human girls, plump as bran muffins, red-haired, freckled, dressed in Virgin-Mary-blue smocks with long-sleeved white blouses, again aged ten years or so. They haven't even sat down on the bench when they charge like tanks into a duet called "Swaying Daffodils." For Daniel Daylight, the daffodils try desperately to sway first this way and then that but can't quite do it; to him, first they bang around, then leap about, then bang around some more, until they just droop from exhaustion, stems half bent over, heads hanging down, sad daffodils, unlucky plants. They are next, he, Daniel Daylight, and, she, Jenny Dean.

Daniel Daylight marches down the aisle that separates the Indian section of the huge auditorium from the white section. Jenny Dean joins him from the other side. Two hundred and fifty human people look at them as with the eyes of alligators, Daniel Daylight thinks, for he can feel them on his back, cold and wet and gooey. He shudders, then climbs the steps that lead to the stage and the upright piano, following the eight-year-old white girl Jenny Dean in her fluffy pink cotton dress with the white lace collar and shoulders that puff out like popcorn. They reach the piano. They sit down. From where he sits, Daniel Daylight can see Mr. Tipper looking up at him with eyes, he is sure of it, that say, "Go on, you can do it." Only twenty-five or so Indian people, mostly women, sit scattered around him, also looking up at him but with dark eyes that say nothing. On the room's other side, he can see the eyes that, to him, are screaming, "No, you can't; you can't do it. You can't do it at all." Feeling Jenny Dean's naked left arm pressing up against his own black-suited, white-shirted arm, he takes his right hand off his lap, raises it above the keyboard of the Heintzman upright. He can hear a gasp from the audience. Then he is sure he can hear the white side whispering to one another, "What's he doing there, little Indian boy, brown-skinned boy? His people cannot vote; therefore they are not human. Non-human boys do *not* play the piano, not in public, and not with human girls." Daniel Daylight, however, will have none of it. Instead, gentle as snow on spruce boughs at night, he lets fall his right hand right on the C-major chord.

Water-like, limpid, calm as silence, the chords for "Hearts and Flowers" begin their journey. Placed with care, every note of them, on the keyboard by Daniel Daylight, they float, float like mist. The bass sneaks in, the melody begins. Playing octaves, Jenny Dean's hands begin at the two Cs above middle C, arc up to the G in a curve smooth and graceful, then waft back down to the F, move on down to the E, and thence to the D, skip down to the B and thus swerve back, up to the C whence they had started. The melody pauses, Daniel Daylight's series of major chords billow out to fill the silence, Jenny Dean's elegant melody resumes its journey. In love with the god sound, Daniel Daylight sends his/her* waves, as prayer from the depths of his heart, the depths of his being, right across the vast auditorium, right through the flesh and bone and blood of some three hundred people, through the walls of the room, beyond them, north across the Moostoos River, through Waskeechoos, north to the Watson Lake Indian Residential School and thus through the lives of the two hundred Indian children who live there, then northward and northward and northward until the sound waves wash up on the shores, and the islands, of vast Minstik Lake. And there, deep inside the blood of Daniel Daylight, where lives Minstik Lake and all her people, Daniel Daylight sees his parents, Cheechup Daylight and his wife, Adelaide, walking up the hill to the little voting booth at the little wooden church that overlooks the northern extremity of beautiful, extraordinary Minstik Lake with its ten thousand islands. And Daniel Daylight, with the magic that he weaves like a tiny little master, *wills* his parents to walk right past Father Roy in his great black cassock and into the booth with their worn yellow pencils. And there they vote. Frozen into place by the prayer of Daniel Daylight and his "flower," Jenny Dean, Father Roy can do nothing, least of all stop Cheechup Daylight and his wife, Adelaide, from becoming human.

Receiving, on stage, his trophy beside Jenny Dean from a human man in black suit, shirt, and tie—Mayor Bill Hicks of Prince William, has explained Mr. Tipper—Daniel Daylight beams at the crowd that fills, for the most part, the Kiwanis Auditorium in downtown Prince William,

Manitoba. Both sides are standing, the Indian side with its two dozen people, the white side with its 250. And they are clapping. And clapping and clapping. Some of them, in fact, are crying, white and Indian, human and...well, they don't look non-human any more, not from where stands exulting—and weeping—the Cree Indian, *human* pianist Daniel Daylight.

Daniel Daylight sits inside Mr. Tipper's travelling car. It is cold—not cold, though, like outside, of this fact Daniel Daylight is quite certain. He looks out through the window on his right and, as always, sees white forest rushing by; maybe rabbits will bound past on that snowbank in the trees, he sits thinking. Snow falling gently, it looks, to Daniel Daylight, like he is being hurtled through the heart of a giant snowflake. In his black-trousered lap, meanwhile, rests his trophy, a ten-inch-tall golden angel with wings outspread and arms wide open, beaming up at her winner through the glow of the travelling car's dashboard lights. On the radio, the music has stopped and people living in the east of the country, explains Mr. Tipper, are discussing a matter that takes Daniel Daylight completely by surprise: the Indian people of Canada, it seems, were given, that day, the 31st of March, 1960, the right to vote in federal elections, in their own country.

"You see?" Daniel Daylight says to Mr. Tipper, his English, and his confidence, having grown quite nicely in just two months. "We are human. I knew it. And you know why I knew it, Mr. Tipper?"

"Why, Daniel Daylight?"

"Because I played it."

*Like all North American Aboriginal languages (that I know of anyway, and there are a lot, fifty-two in Canada alone!), the Cree language has no gender. According to its structure, therefore, we are all, in a sense, he/shes, as is all of nature (trees, vegetation, even rocks), as is God, one would think. That is why I, for one, have so much trouble just thinking in the English language—because it is a language that is, first and foremost, "motored," as it were, by a theology/mythology that is "monotheistic" in structure, a structure where there is only one God and that god is male and male only. Other world systems are either "polytheistic" or "pantheistic" in structure, having, for instance (now or in the past, as in ancient Greece), room for gods who are female or even male/female, systems where all of nature, including sound, just for instance, simply "bristles," as it were, with divinity.

Seelim's Flowers

Eric Moore

"Bring in the maintainer t'do this road up by the dam here. Let's say it's the *Champion*."

"It can't be the *Champion*, the *Champion's* yellow. It'd have t'be the *Atlas*—like they got out in Athol." The two boys were crouched on the outskirts of a miniature town they had constructed in a pile of coarse, pebble-strewn sand. Parked at various locations around the town were several digging, hauling, and scooping machines comprising an impressive fleet of plastic construction equipment: an orange dump truck (mate to the maintainer), a cement truck, steam-shovel and bulldozer (these three bright yellow), and a red fire truck with white ladders and a rubber hose that actually sprayed water—sometimes. There was also a green, cast-metal *John Deere* tractor which was missing a front wheel, but it was used only sparingly to cultivate a scraggly patch of dandelions on the far reaches of the town near the foot of a ratty Manitoba maple.

Here and there, tall stalks of goat's beard poked up through the mound of dirty sand. This concerned the boys not a whit. Roadways and houses were built around and between the goat's beard and where this proved impossible, they simply hauled the sinewy, grey-green stems out by their roots and tossed them over the hedge into the neighbouring yard. The few plants that remained provided an aesthetically pleasing accent to the otherwise barren desert landscape of the model town, towering over it like strange, yellow-topped trees.

"Okay, this road's ready. Bring'er in and let's have some mix." One of the boys stretched his arm out over the town square and manoeuvred the big yellow cement truck along the freshly levelled road to the site of the town's new water reservoir. He backed the truck into position and began to turn a crank on its side. The big drum spun around and concrete flowed down a black chute into cardboard forms that the boys had re-barred with dead twigs collected from beneath the ratty maple.

The concrete was of the boys' own devising. The recipe was two parts sand to two parts water to three parts all-purpose flour. (Several test batches had to be mixed up before the boys finally hit upon the proper ratio of ingredients and the contents of the red and white-checked flour tin which sat next to the molasses jar in the bottom cupboard of the tiny kitchen in the little frame house behind which the model town was being constructed had been severely depleted.)

Robin Hood Ready-Mix—as the boys called their flour-based mud—looked and behaved much like the real thing in the initial stages of pouring and filling of forms. However—much to the dismay of the two young engineers—it took forever to set up and structures made with it were prone to severe cracking and crumbling. Given these defects, *Robin Hood Ready-Mix* was probably *not* the best choice for the construction of a reservoir. Still, the town needed a reliable water supply and, as the boys dared not risk another *teaspoon* of flour on further experimentation, the forms for the new dam were filled and trowelled smooth with a discarded popsicle stick. The mixer on the back of the yellow cement truck was hosed-out and, construction for the moment at a standstill, the two boys sat back to contemplate life.

Now these were not bad boys. In fact, if you asked any one of the other residents of the small village into which fate had decided to plunk this pair of juvenile urban developers, what they were like, most everyone would have said they were good boys. They spoke respectfully to their elders, did reasonably well in school and always marched in the fall fair parade—one of them even attended *St. Stephen's on the Hill* every Sunday morning. No, these were decent boys from upstanding, hard-working families. There was *one* thing about these two boys however: they were both nine years old.

That was the problem on this shimmering, July afternoon as monarch butterflies fluttered amongst the milkweed and the heat from the sun lifted the scent of earth and grass and other growing things up into the air. These two boys weren't evil. These boys weren't delinquents or bad seeds or trash. These boys were nine years old. *That* was the problem.

As the day wore on it became hotter and hotter. The boys lolled about the edges of the sandy little town and tormented one another with tales of fantastic and utterly unattainable refreshment. The boy with the buck teeth and kiss-curl forelock waxed eloquent on the wondrous properties of a magical drinking fountain which spewed, not water, but an endless stream of ice cold *Coca-Cola* while the boy with the freckles and chronic cough spun an enticing tale about a never-ending box of grape-flavoured *Mr. Frostees*.

Presently, the boy with the teeth and the curl got to his

feet and, setting one foot gingerly into the centre of town, grasped a goat's beard-tree with both hands and tore it from the school yard.

"Hey, what're ya doin' ya dork?" said the other boy, sounding not very concerned at all.

"I've been lookin' at it. Didn't look right. There's no trees in our schoolyard."

"Yea, I guess so." The freckled boy coughed his three quick little dry coughs and went back to studying the horse fly that was probing the knee of his blue jeans. His friend filled the hole in the schoolyard with the toe of his black and white running shoe and turned to fling the goat's beard over the hedge. Just as he was about to toss it he paused, let his arm fall slowly back to his side, and stood staring into the next yard.

"Look at that old coot," he said, mostly to himself. The "old coot" was Seelim Starks. Seelim was well known around the village for two reasons: first, his age. He was reckoned by most folks to be somewhere near one hundred. Ab Chapman, who owned the butcher shop and general store next door to Seelim and knew him as well as anybody, maintained he was actually ninety-three. Seelim's second claim to fame was his garden, or rather, his *gardens*. Seelim Starks had the most beautiful flower gardens of anyone in the entire village—some said the entire township. From the first warm days of April, when spring begins to tease with hints of the coming summer, through to the killing frosts of late October, Seelim was out working his flower gardens.

He was a small man; not tiny or frail, but small in the way that old age can take a large, robust man and shrink him. Untold hours out of doors had turned Seelim's skin the colour and texture of calf and he walked all stooped over, as if, after years of repeatedly bending and straightening over his beloved flowers, he'd decided to save himself half the effort. His face was all bony points and hollows, little more than a skull over which the skin appeared to have been stretched a tad too tightly. A great, curved beak of a nose marked the centre point of his ancient countenance, and pinched to its bridge, a pair of golden, wire-rimmed spectacles focused sunken, watery blue eyes onto petal, bloom, and bud.

There was no mistaking Seelim Starks. If you failed to recognize the face or the angled, shuffling gait, you'd know him by his clothes. Seelim always wore the same clothes. Not the same *style* of clothes, or different articles of apparel which were identical; he always wore the *same* clothes: a frayed, green cotton shirt, buttoned to the throat, under faded, blue bib-overalls, and over these a dirty, grey woollen sweater with the elbows out and most of the buttons missing. A Chinese-style straw hat with a wide, decaying brim and fraying chin-string crowned the gaunt, leathery head and on his feet were the cheapest of rubber-soled canvas shoes—so worn and thin that they looked in danger of crumbling away with his very next step. Thusly attired did Seelim Starks tend his flower gardens. In fact, thusly attired did Seelim Starks live out every day of the entire year. Even in the dead of winter, when day-lily and delphinium and cornflower were locked in frozen slumber, Seelim's costume never varied. No matter how deep the snow or how bitter the wind, Seelim Starks went out into the world in straw and cotton, denim and canvas.

Not that he went out very often. Nor did he go very far. Every few weeks Seelim would make a short trek from his house to Chapman's store for tea and oatmeal and marmalade. He would pick his way slowly along the icy sidewalk, head down, studying the terrain, placing one foot carefully in front of the other. He looked for all the world like a great, drab shore bird that has tarried too long on a favourite beach and was now prisoner of the ice and snow. His only concession to the cold—and it had to be extreme— was a shabby, brown, military greatcoat that he had brought home from the trenches of France.

Now I must tell you that a few of the people in the village thought Seelim something of a recluse. Some even called him a hermit. And while most didn't go that far, they did agree that he was somewhat, well, *stand-offish* was a word that got tossed around a fair bit. And there were rumours about the roots of this anti-social behaviour. It was the usual sort of romantic nonsense that people in small villages are particularly fond of spinning about members of their community that they deem odd or different but don't really know anything about. (There is a law of physics which states: *if a void exists it must be filled by something.* The law of village life states: *if the facts aren't known they must be invented.*) In Seelim's case there was talk of a pretty young wife, struck down in the prime of life by a terrible disease. Or, depending on who was telling the story, a pretty young wife who died in child birth—the child with her—or a pretty young wife who ran off with a *Bovril* salesman. At any rate, however this comely young woman came to take her leave, her departure left Seelim with a broken heart and the will to do nothing more with his life than grow breathtakingly beautiful flowers in her memory.

The truth of the matter was that Seelim had indeed been married, for forty odd years, to a plain, dour little woman named Prudence. They'd worked their tiny farm together until 1962 when Prudence died an unremarkable death, the result of complications arising from a common cold. She was buried in the Cherry Valley cemetery and Seelim hardly ever thought about her. *That* was the long and short of Seelim Starks's quite ordinary life: he'd been young once, married a woman he wasn't quite sure he'd ever loved, she'd died, and now he was old. And while it was true that he didn't go out of his way to engage people in conversation, his reticence had nothing at all to do with the death of his wife. Seelim didn't actively seek people out for idle chit-chat because, at ninety-three, he'd long ago said all that he had to say about anything important to anybody worth saying it to—at least that's the way Seelim saw it. And if the truth be told, most of the people in the village didn't exactly go out of their way to engage Seelim in conversation because—the way *they* saw it—he was just an old man who pottered about in his flower beds all day. What could *he* possibly have to say that would be worth listening to?

The simple fact of the matter was that Seelim Starks was a very old man with a remarkably verdant thumb who just happened to love flowers more than he loved people. Flowers were all that he cared about, all that he was interested in, all that he ever thought of. The true love of Seelim Starks's life wasn't dead and mouldering in a grave; she was vibrant and bright and singing all around him. She was the golden spirit of growth and green things that you feel like a tingle of electricity on warm spring mornings. She was the sweet breath of the creator that sometimes hides in the folds of a summer breeze and leaves you happy and sad and wondering after it has passed. She was the life-giving magic of nature herself manifest in the flowers of his gardens.

"Look at that old coot," the boy with the curl and teeth said again, the goat's beard drooping in his fist.

"Who?" asked the other boy, squashing the horse fly and getting up to stand beside his friend.

"Him. Old man Starks. All he ever does is fart around with those flowers. Jeez." The boys watched as Seelim trundled a wheelbarrow full of rotted cow manure from a pile behind his barn over to a wisteria vine that was rambling in bright profusion over the back wall of his house. (Wisteria was generally considered too delicate to survive the village winters but Seelim had the touch. He'd planted the vine on the south side of the house where it was sheltered from the winter winds and in early November, when he was certain the vine had gone to sleep, he would cover the bed with a thick thatch of straw.

But the key to the seemingly magical success of Seelim's wisteria vine was fish tea: an especially pungent and potent brew of guts, heads and tails that Seelim boiled up in a five gallon metal bucket. After the tea had steeped and cooled, Seelim tucked the bucket away in a dark corner of his little barn and covered it with a burlap sack. Then, at regular intervals throughout the spring and summer, he would remove the burlap, skim the maggots from the surface of the festering brew and treat the wisteria to three or four generous dippers-full of this wonderfully ripe tonic).

It had taken several years of fussing to get the vine established, but now it was growing vigorously and had spread out to cover the entire wall, footing to gutter. Its flowers were so lush and plentiful that from where the boys were standing it looked as if someone had painted the red brick wall a delicate shade of mauve.

The boys watched as Seelim heaped manure around the foot of the plant with a short-handled spade. The freckled boy got off a trio of shallow coughs and nudged his friend.

"Hey, wonder what smells worse; the cow shit or Seelim?" They both erupted in peels of laughter.

"Yea! I'll bet he never washes. He wears the same friggin' clothes all the time."

"Yea! And he's nothin' but bones. Like a skeleton walkin' around for Chrissakes. Why doesn't he eat somethin'? I heard he's got tons of money." Seelim scooped the last of the manure from the wheelbarrow and worked it gently into the earth with the point of the spade. His movements were slow and meditative.

(Now, had the pastor of St. Stephen's happened by at that particular moment and caught a glimpse of Seelim tending to his wisteria, and had the pastor an eye for nuance and detail, he might have been reminded of the women who served on the altar guild of the church. He might have recognized in Seelim's tender nurturing of the vine the same reverence and sense of wonder apparent in the faces of the women as they lovingly cleaned and polished the brass candlesticks and the silver cross and the golden chalice of their Lord's holy table.

He might have. But on this particular July afternoon the pastor was tucked away in the air-conditioned comfort of the rectory study, hard at work on a sermon he had titled, *Paul's Letter to the Corinthians: Is There Postage Due?* And the other residents of the village seemed to have said, "To hell with it," and gone *en masse* in search of shade, fan, ice, pool, beach, breeze, beer, *anything* that might take the edge off the blistering heat. There was no one to witness Seelim's loving devotions that afternoon save two small boys watching intently across a hedge of yellow-flowered honeysuckle).

Seelim set the spade in the wheelbarrow and stood gazing at the wisteria. His eyes followed the twisting, many-fingered vine as far up the brick wall as his rusty back would allow. He reached out with his hand, gently touched one of the delicate flowers, stroked the rough bark of the vine and smiled. It wasn't a self-satisfied kind of smile, one that says, *"I grew this. This is here because of me."* It was the sort of smile that comes now and then when your hands are in good earth and you breathe in the rich, musty aroma of decay and regeneration. Or you see a robin bouncing across a dew-sparkled lawn. It was the smile of a man taking pleasure in the vitality and beauty of another living thing.

"What the hell is he grinnin' at?" growled the curl and the teeth.

"Who knows. He's crazy. He probably thinks the flowers talk to him. Hey, maybe that creeper told him a joke!" The boys snorted again and watched as Seelim made his way slowly across the yard, trailing the wheelbarrow behind him. The moment he disappeared into the barn the boy who'd been clutching the goat's beard hurled it across the hedge and pushed his way through into Seelim's yard.

"Hey, what're ya doin' ya dork!?" his friend whispered loudly, this time sounding very much concerned.

"C'mon!" cried the other boy. "Let's teach the old coot a lesson." (Later, when it was all over and he was asked why he'd done it, what on earth had possessed him, the boy with the freckles and the chronic cough had no words for it all. He couldn't begin to describe the strange feeling that had come over him as he'd watched his friend charging across the yard. He couldn't explain the sense of excitement he'd felt as he too broke through the honeysuckle. He couldn't put into words how he knew—even before he saw his friend pick up the oak-handled pruning shears leaning against the side of the barn—that something dangerous was going to happen or why he wanted so very much to be a part of it).

The boy with the teeth and the curl snatched up the shears and ran to a flowerbed on the far side of the yard. Although the shears were large and heavy, Seelim kept them well oiled and they opened and closed easily. Seelim also kept the shears very sharp. The boy paused. He was feeling rather light-headed and his breath was coming in short, anxious puffs. The shears quivered for a moment in his hands, and then he began. Lofty, multi-flowered hollyhocks—lavender, yellow, and white—tumbled in upon each other and lay jumbled like gigantic matchsticks in the middle of the bed. The boy marvelled at how easily the shears sliced through the fibrous stalks.

"C'mon!" he yelled to his friend, "cut some!"

The boys raced to the back of the yard.

"Here!" cried the teeth and the curl, his eyes shining as he pushed the shears into his friend's hands, "do it!" They were standing in front of a large rose bush, its lush, green foliage almost obscured by clusters of fat, scarlet blooms.

"Do it! Do it! Give'm a haircut!" The freckled boy split open the shears, thrust them into the heart of the bush and in a frenzy of scissoring, reduced it to a heap of red and green litter. The blue delphiniums were the next to fall, and after the delphiniums, the pink-petaled and yellow-domed cone flowers. The boys whooped and squealed as they raced from bed to bed.

(Had the pastor happened by at *that* particular moment, and had the pastor been a man of a more *fundamental* persuasion, a man who believed that Satan was out and about on a regular basis, walking to and fro upon the face of the earth conducting business with the most unlikely customers, the phrase *unholy din* might have popped into his head. And he might have wondered at the niggling prickle of fear that he suddenly felt creep along his spine and raise up the hairs on the back of his neck. He might have; for there was something in the tenor of the clamour and wail arising from Seelim's back yard; a certain *quality*, a *tone* running just below the surface of the general hue and cry; something subtle yet unmistakable and *most* unsettling.)

Seelim had just removed the burlap from the metal bucket and was preparing to ladle fish tea into a tomato can when he heard the first shriek. He emerged into the sunlight in time to see the boys lay waste to a stand of purple monk's hood growing in a bed in the centre of the yard. He stood frozen, gaping, not quite able to comprehend what he was seeing: two young boys, one of whom was brandishing what appeared to be his very own pruning shears, were tearing around his yard like crazed banshees and all about them was death and destruction: the rose bush, the hollyhocks—everywhere he looked—the day lilies, the delphiniums. In every corner of the yard there was waste and ruin. He continued to stare, dumbfounded, as the boys finished off a clump of snow-white coral bells and ran off toward the rear of the house. It was only when Seelim realized they were headed for the wisteria that he found his voice.

"Hey!" he croaked, for a croak was all that the shock and his aged lungs would allow him to muster. "Hey! what are you doing!? What in God's name are you doing!?" The boys had just reached the wisteria when the sound of Seelim's voice brought them up short. They turned and saw the old man hobbling across the yard, waving his arms and calling for them to stop.

"Jeez, here he comes," gasped the boy with the buck-teeth and the kiss-curl forelock, "let's get outta here!"

"One more!" screeched the boy with the freckles and the cough, the rapture of the slaughter making him giddy. "He doesn't know who we are. One more!" He wrenched the shears from his friend's hands and turning to face Seelim, called out in a voice shrill and quavering with emotion.

"Hey, ya old fart! I don't think this thing'll be tellin' ya any more jokes!" He turned back to the house, opened the shears, and with a vicious stroke, cut clean through the main branch of the wisteria vine. The teeth and the curl howled, the other boy threw down the shears and both of them went crashing back through the hedge and disappeared into the heat of the afternoon.

Seelim had almost reached the house when the boy killed the wisteria. The blades of the shears passing through the vine also seemed to sever something in Seelim for the jerking, bobbing shuffle that had propelled him across the lawn faltered, sputtered, and then petered out completely. He staggered the last few steps to the house and stood staring at the vine. Its flowers were still lush and beautiful, shimmering brightly in the afternoon sun, seemingly unaware that they were already dead.

After a moment, Seelim turned and hobbled back to the barn. He took a pitchfork, shovel, and rake from their wooden pegs on the wall, placed them in the wheelbarrow and returned outside. He went first to the rear of the yard and scooped up the mountain of red and green potpourri which only minutes ago had been a magnificent rose bush. He moved next to the delphiniums and hollyhocks, cutting the long, slender stalks into regular lengths with his pocket-knife.

Seelim went about his work in a slow, methodical manner. He felt no anger. He didn't question why the boys had done it, he knew what boys could do. He felt no grief; save one, tiny twinge when he pulled the wisteria vine from the wall. Seelim knew that things happened in this world which made no sense and for which there were no answers. He'd killed men in a pointless war. His wife, a woman he'd married simply because it had seemed like the thing to do, had caught a cold and three weeks later she was dead. There was no reason for it. And there was no reason, no logical explanation why the boys had cut down his flowers— they'd just done it.

The only thought that occupied the old man's mind that

hot, summer afternoon as he wheeled the barrow full of brightly coloured, lifeless debris to the compost heap behind his tiny barn was one of time; time measured in the passing of a day's work into weeks, and weeks into seasons. Summer would soon turn to fall and then there would be another winter to get through. Time. Precious time. That was all that Seelim could think about as he closed up the barn and limped across the lawn to the back door of his house. He knew that he could make the gardens beautiful again. Was pretty sure even that he could bring the wisteria back, but it was going to take time. How much did he have left? Would there be *enough time* for him to make it all right again?

The miniature town lay in ruins; the walls of the water reservoir smashed beyond repair, houses and roadways obliterated. A goat's beard tree, its trunk buckled and bent, rested at a crazy angle against the crumbled walls of the school house. The boys' flight from the carnage in the neighbouring yard had carried them, their small feet trampling and smashing, straight through the middle of the sandy community.

The boy with the kiss curl and the buckteeth made a beeline for an overgrown pasture on the other side of the village. He pushed his way through the long grass until he reached the middle of the field where he lay down and curled himself into a ball. He had a notion that he might somehow hide from what he had done; that the foxtails and the timothy would cover up his terrible deed as easily as they now covered him. If he could just stay hidden long enough he told himself, everything would probably be okay. He hugged himself tighter and began to shake.

The boy with the freckles and the chronic cough ran directly home and shut himself away in his bedroom. He sat on the bed and thought about what had happened. The thrill he'd felt while wielding the shears had vanished, replaced by an almost claustrophobic sense of guilt and dread. At first he tried to make himself believe that everything was going to be all right. Like he'd said, the old man didn't know any of the kids in the village and probably didn't see so well. Heck, he probably didn't have a clue who those two boys were. And besides that, nobody else saw what happened. But even as he thought it he knew it was no good; this was the village; there was *always* somebody else.

He then started to think about the lies that he could tell. He could say he wasn't even around when it happened. That he'd been down at the creek looking for mud turtles. Why, there was no proof it was him no matter what anybody said.

He was still sitting on his bed and hour later, still thinking up alibis, when his mother opened the bedroom door. Her face was ashen and the boy noticed she was trembling. She walked into the room and stood gazing down upon him. She spoke slowly, biting off each word, her voice grim and threatening.

"What, have, you, done? Look at me! What have you *done*!?"

The boy looked into his mother's eyes and began to sob. Deep, anguished sobs of remorse and fear. But mostly he cried out of *frustration*. He was, of course, sorry for what he'd done—and he was *very* afraid of what was going to happen to him. But try as he might, the boy could not understand *why*. He couldn't identify the *thing*; the *urge*, the *desire*, way deep down inside of him that had driven him to act in such a wilful fashion; to do something so cruel and wicked and...*wrong*.

"I don't *know* why I did it mom! I don't *know*!" That

was all the little boy could say on that hot, summer afternoon as he rocked back and forth on his bed, his face buried in the pillow.

"I don't know!" "I don't know!" "I don't know!" And how could he? He was a child. A nine year old boy.

HELEN'S VISIT

Sue Scherzinger

"Insensitive," Helen said. She frowned at the gold-framed picture of her dead husband, Charlie. "They don't care about anyone but themselves. If I don't look after Doreen, they certainly won't. And they're her sisters, you know. They don't even appreciate that I had to buy, with my pension money, your pension money, the hand lotion for her. It gets so dry in the hospital and the sheets are so rough."

Charlie never answered, of course, but it was good of him to listen. Helen heard the hiss of her soup boiling over and she pushed herself up off the sofa and rushed over to the kitchenette but it was too late, she would have to clean the stove now on top of everything.

Helen drizzled the cream into the simmering broth with the carefully sautéed Vidalia onions and shiitake, oyster and button mushrooms, stirring to prevent curdling. It was Doreen's favourite mushroom soup. Helen poured the soup into a heated thermos and put the remainder in a bowl covered with an inverted plate for her own supper later.

"If I didn't have to make soup for her," she said to Charlie, "I'd just have a toast, a piece of cheese and an apple for supper tonight." She sat at the small round table with the pad under the pale blue tablecloth covered with the lacy tablecloth her sister, Hester, had crocheted the year before she died, all protected by the clear plastic. She traced the lacy pattern with her finger and remembered when she, Doreen and Hester would go to teas at the church together. Helen had always loved those little finger sandwiches, especially the pinwheel ones with cream cheese and a cherry. Doreen always liked the craft sale after the tea even though she never bought anything. She always said, "Well, really I could make that for a lot less." But she never did make anything.

Her cuckoo clock, a gift from Charlie that had always irritated her with its hourly chirping, informed her that it was four o'clock. She had half an hour to get ready or she would miss her bus. The soup was ready and the strawberries purchased last summer at the farmer's market and frozen in little bags were thawing in their plastic container. Doreen always loved strawberries. Even now when she usually didn't remember Helen, she always smiled at the strawberries.

Helen fingered her thinning hair back into place. The hairspray from the stylist was still holding for the most part. Tomorrow she would have to wash it. Her hair was so white now but she saw little point in dying it. She put blush on her pale cheeks with their crisscross of fine lines and her pinkest lipstick on her thinning lips. She didn't try to make them look fuller by painting outside the lines like her friend Nan did. She wasn't fooling anyone. Nan was gone now too.

Thinning hair, thinning lips, thinning bony hands with thin skin. Helen was thinned out. It was a cold December day in Sudbury and a good walk to the bus stop. She had to cross Paris, go down Brady and wait for the bus on Minto

St. It wasn't fair that she couldn't just stay home with her afghan around her shoulders, the small afghan she'd made with leftover wool on her right knee that ached so these days and watch her shows (re-runs of *Golden Girls* were on tonight) while she ate her supper.

Doreen's sisters never helped her eat though. The St. Joseph's staff was kind but too busy to take the time for an old woman who didn't even know who you were anymore. Doreen's stroke had been devastating. Lucky she had Helen to feed her and get her moisturizer and comb her hair.

Helen arrived at the bus stop with her insulated bag of food with time to spare. The shelter offered small relief from the biting cold. At least the office girls waiting for their buses home were friendly and consoling. You'd think Doreen's sisters would at least have offered to pick Helen up on a day like this but they were so selfish. Helen really didn't know if she could handle this all winter. And now the hospital staff was talking about moving Doreen to another facility. A hospice. A home for the dying across town. Two buses to get there. Helen's small shoulders rounded forward at the thought.

The nurses were always happy to see Helen. She was cheerful and helpful. They had a smile, a small hug and a few kind words for her each day. Today though, as Helen stepped off the elevator, their smiles seemed weak and distracted. Sherri, the young nurse who most often helped Doreen, looked up as Helen approached.

The tall blond woman stood slowly, tucking a stray hair back under her cap. "Helen," she said. "I need to talk to you, dear." She took Helen's hand and led her into the small room at the back of the nurses' station. The room reserved for bad news.

"She's already been moved, hasn't she?" Helen said. It would be a long trip tonight. Three buses to get there now.

Then two back. Helen wouldn't get her supper until after 7:30 and she would feel nauseous by then. She was getting angry at the sisters for not having told her before she left, especially on a day like this.

"Helen," Sherri said softly as she covered the thin cold hand with her own warm full hand. "Doreen hasn't been moved, dear. I'm sorry. She's passed on. We went in to check on her this afternoon and she was gone. I'm sorry. We thought her family would have told you."

Gone? Dead? Helen felt a guilty sense of relief. Her first thought was how she could sit with her afghans and eat a simple supper tomorrow night. It was better for Doreen. There hadn't been anything left of her. She wouldn't have wanted to carry on like that. No sadness for a good long life. No need to feel guilty but she did.

"Helen," Sherri said, tears in her eyes, "are you going to be okay? Is there someone I can call for you? Someone to get you?"

"No," Helen said. "There is no one left to call. I'll be fine." The nurses all gave her a small hug and told her how they would miss her visits.

Helen sat on her rose-print wingback chair, afghans in place, television on with the volume turned up so she could take out her hearing aids and still hear the show. Her ears got so itchy. This was what she'd wanted. It had been three weeks of her new routine of caring just for herself. It was what she'd wanted. No one to look after. No obligations. No one to visit. She wondered what the office girls at the bus stop were talking about. She thought of the busy, friendly nurses. She looked over at Charlie, Doreen and Hester smiling at her from on the wall.

"Insensitive," she said as a tear rolled down her blushless cheek onto the thin pale lips.

RASPBERRY

Kathy Ashby

Alone, leaning over the steering wheel, I pronounce, "Sarah." I watch the spittle hit the windshield as I yell, "Please...remember my name is Sarah." My mother doesn't know my name. The honking of cars up ahead drowns out my voice. Every Friday, 5:05 p.m., I negotiate my red Honda Civic through traffic congestion, and head out of the city. I keep my eyes ahead while I recite a poem, the poem she taught me. "Life has earthquakes, droughts and storms, even thorns. Watch weather flips. Cruel words take flight from lips..." In the distance I spot the exit ramp. I pull away from the main route, my route home to husband cooking Kraft dinner for kids. Instead I head north to Sunset Acres— her Home. I know my husband will give the kids a treat, a bath and pack them off after a bedtime story. He'll wait for me to have a late supper, just the two of us, with wine and later a movie, our treat. I won't be able to enjoy the treat or the whole weekend off unless I get the visit in. I must see her before the weekend officially starts. "When summer's heat clings to pores, anger soars..." Guilt would not let me have it any other way.

Many Fridays Nurse Jane has said, "It's really up to

you Dear," her sad blue eyes bathing me in comfort. She is a good nurse. I know this because I remember she told me once "Your mom," she said happily, "Likes raspberry Jell-O." I remember how my body swooned towards Nurse Jane telling her about the poem, my favourite times with Mom making jam, jellies and pies, our respite from the onslaught of her early Alzheimer's. Lost in her mind, I don't get to say goodbye. "Sunshine or summer rain, a welcome gift brings ecstasy, first of season, recurring for no reason, merry, bursting joy, red raspberry..."

"Lovely."

"Thanks," I said to Nurse Jane, bowing my head, keeping my chin down for a moment as if issuing gratefulness from the bottom of my heart. When I looked up then, I saw Nurse Jane smile.

I don't bother to lock my car at Sunset Acres. I wipe my brow; blink my eyes searching. I see Nurse Jane waving from just inside the wide open doors of the Sunroom, a look of concern on her face. "She hardly touched her supper," Nurse Jane calls out as I pass. She shakes her head, back and forth 3 times, our code for a *bad* day. It tells me all. No improvement. Don't expect anything. Your mother won't recognize you so don't get your hopes up.

With a polite wave of thanks I then nod my chin towards my mother's small shape and the extra chair placed for me. I glance at my watch, 7 o'clock. Almost nighttime for the folks here. I spy my mother's old bones against the reclining back of a lawn chair as usual, looking as flat as the small blanket on her lap. How can she be cold on a day like today? I walk over, listening to my shoes rustle the parched grass.

I know it was Nurse Jane who let my mother sit way off, close to the edge of the Sunset Acres property. I know it was her who helped my mother walk as near to the woods as was allowed. There is always a risk of wandering and getting lost with the residents but we both know how my mother insists every night, anyway.

I slip into the chair with the easy way of joining my mother on Fridays, a way that Nurse Jane and I came up with. I let my bag drop behind me out of sight, my purse with my driver's license, social insurance number, and credit card out of the way; it is the paraphernalia I carry with me that identifies me. I try not to slump. If I just sit without saying, "Hi Mom," then I avoid the risk of her frustration at not being able to recognize me. Nurse Jane had said, "It's like you're one of the staff then, just someone to sit with her, someone who might reach out and take her pulse."

I welcome the breeze that comes with scent of summer dryness, petal, stamen, seed and earth. I do not reach out and take her hand just yet.

"Weather's coming," I sigh.

My mom looks up with attention. I see her eyes scan my face, like she is looking at a page from a book. I feel her read every line from left to right, from my top to my bottom, but I am not a character in the story that she knows.

I turn away. The earth has shifted axis, the rays of sun dipping below the underbrush to my right. Branches arc in surrender to their dry God. The leaves bob and sway with new surprise. Under cool green shade a spot of red gleams very brightly. I say out loud, "The highlight, like a curve of gold, foils the berry in a crown of glory." I see my mother's head lift. My body stands up quickly. I sense her eyes following my swift but careful move. I push back undergrowth to expose the moist ball of trapped bubbles. I pluck it with the skill built from childhood. I cup my palm and return to my seat facing Mother. I see her eyes follow mine to my slowly unfolding fingers. I will give her the gentleness of soft sun. Her eyes hold on to the glistening fruit that sails towards her, through the air into her opened lips. I see her eyes pop as she closes her mouth. I see them flood with memory, drinking from her heart. I watch the zing stretch across her face. Tears roll down her cheeks. She puts out her arms. I fill them. Cheek to wet warm cheek, I feel her swallow, "Sarah."

In one white shining moment of peace, because of a raspberry, I am no longer orphaned.

THE WATCHER

Margo Little

The day it happened, Sam was a bit more quiet than usual. Only by looking back and rehashing the events of that day did we admit that to ourselves. We hadn't really given it much thought at the time. Nobody had tried to draw him out of his silence. It was none of our business. In Janet Cove we mostly mind our own business.

I say mostly, because there is a notable exception. One particular group traditionally scrutinizes everyone's affairs. They are known as the watchers. When I first moved to the Cove to recuperate from my accident, I didn't know what to make of these gossipy old codgers. But after awhile, I became an informal member of the watcher society. My slouched shoulders and exaggerated limp show them I have paid my dues. They seem to accept me even though I am half their age.

It's hard to describe just what the watchers do. Mostly, they keep an eye on things. The brigade is made up of George, a farmer driven from his inhospitable land by drink and debt; Ken, a former fisherman whose main catch is now tainted with mercury, and Walter, a timberman long disabled by a falling tree.

Paul is also a regular. He worked as a heavy equipment operator at the dolomite quarry until the air pollution destroyed his lungs. Too many impaired charges have made Ernie a permanent fixture with the watchers. He used to be a long-haul trucker, but now he is grounded without a licence.

And, of course, there was Sam. He was the point man with the watchers; we looked to him to set the tone of the day. He could always be counted on to reveal a tantalizing piece of news that the local press wouldn't touch. Sam would rage about the injustices he had suffered and the others would join in the lament.

"I sold my soul to the company store for thirty years," he would complain. "And all I've got to show for it is a bum back and peanuts to live on. This country owes me more than that."

When Sam was among us, there were no sacred cows. Everyone was fair game. He had a way of cutting through the hypocrisy and coming to the defence of the dispossessed. The most popular target for attack was the Workers' Compensation Board. Every man had a horror story to tell about broken promises, bureaucratic red tape and paltry pensions.

The watchers are as much a part of the scenery in Janet Cove as the ice shacks in winter and the sailboats in summer. It took me a while to get into the rhythm of their routine, but after a while it became second nature.

We meet at the Cove's only restaurant every morning at ten and in the late afternoon we rendezvous at the village bake shop. Here in the protective circle of the brotherhood, we gulp bottomless cups of coffee and grumble about everything from free trade to freezing temperatures. Companionship helps to dull the ache of gout, arthritis, emphysema and boredom.

We are all fighting the same enemy. We pass judgment on governments at all levels and analyse the state of the economy until the waitress gets tired of refilling our cups. We skewer crooked politicians as well as the biased referees who are costing us the Stanley cup this year.

But we laugh, too. That's what keeps us going. In mid-January, Lord knows, we need to keep our sense of humour. George has a good joke about the cop who got caught with his pants down. Ken has the latest on the affair between the mayor's wife and the insurance man. Sam is intent on roasting our newly elected Member of Parliament.

I was drawn to Sam from the beginning. Looking back, I guess I was impressed with his bulldog demeanour and feisty attitude. I needed to be with people who knew the secrets to survival.

I came to the small lakeside community to give myself some breathing space in my battle with the bottle. In recent months I have gained a modest reputation as a nature photographer and I've been asked to exhibit some of my work during tourist season.

To the watchers, however, I am just "the guy with the Achilles heel problem." They tend to ignore my frequent jaunts to the escarpment to catch the early morning light. They don't have much patience for artistic types.

"Hey, Graham, better be careful you don't fall off the bluff," Sam teases me. "One of these days that gimpy leg of yours will give out when you least expect it and all we'll have left is your pictures on the wall to remember you by."

His comments don't bother me. It could be worse. I could be hanging out at the Legion (or "the zoo," as it is known to the locals). The younger guys congregate at that smoky watering hole, but I can't handle the alcohol any more, so I make myself at home with the reluctant retirees. I hope to learn something about how to live from these old men.

But Sam couldn't show me how. He could rave on and on about the dirty deal he got from the mining company after his injury. He could write scathing indictments of capitalism in letters to the editor and he could harp for hours on the corruption of the town council. He could get all fired up about the money spent on facilities for the tourists while local youth are neglected. But he couldn't provide the antidote to cynicism that I crave.

Sam used the shotgun approach for everything. He blasted the sheriff, the game warden, and the town clerk with equal venom. The other watchers were spellbound by his belligerence and his ability to zero in on a target with ruthless accuracy. Sam was hard on everyone, but, now I understand, he was even harder on himself.

I don't say much at first. I just sort of listen and observe. As an outsider, I don't want to breach any of the unspoken rules of the Cove. In my struggle to hang on to sobriety, I have to guess at what's normal. I look to the watchers for cues. I search their faces for the insights and the wisdom I assume comes with age. I am hoping to learn how to deal with disappointment and loneliness. But it takes all my energy to keep their bitterness from creeping into my bones.

When I do join in the conversation, I watch my language, because they have visible contempt for "bleeding hearts" and "educated fools." Always I am on the fringes, part of the group, yet apart from it, watching. I am watching for signs that the wait is justified. I am watching for something to strengthen my resolve, something to make it all worthwhile.

Why I looked to Sam for that reinforcement, I don't know. Perhaps it was because the others did. But he let us all down in the end. Before our eyes he became more subdued, more resigned to the futility of the struggle.

Despair settled in as cold and as crushing as the ice floes in the bay. He was our fearless crusader against injustice. Why couldn't he keep the faith?

In retrospect, I know we all saw him shrivelling and withdrawing into himself. But we chose to protect ourselves and watch him drown. It would be too easy to follow him into the sea of despair, too easy to let go of our own fragile life preservers. We kept on treading water and let him slip away. No one had the resources or the courage to buoy him up.

With Sam gone, we can still work up moral outrage about the antics of some politicians, but the punch is missing. More than ever I am alert to the undercurrents of life in Janet Cove; I am aware of the unspoken signals. Behind the stoic masks of the watchers, I begin to discern the powerlessness of old men past their prime, of old men shunted out to pasture, of old men cursing their fate.

I begin to drift.

I do photography when I am on the edge. Instead of reaching for the bottle, I take to the hills and fields around the Cove. I look to the clouds, to the waters of Lake Huron, to the silent bluffs for answers.

Those answers evaded Sam and leave us grappling with confusion and guilt.

"It wasn't as if his heart just gave out," George mutters as we convene after the wake. "We could have lived with that. But, no, he had to go and bail out like that."

We settle in for coffee as usual. "He sure didn't look like himself," George continues, loosening his tie. "The new undertaker seems to wipe all the character out of a man's face. I hardly knew that face."

Walter replays the scenario over and over in his mind. "Did I say something to hurt his feelings? I don't recall him mentioning anything upsetting that day."

Ken is equally perplexed. "He seemed to have a lot of fight left in him. You just never know, do ya?"

There is much shuffling of feet under the table and nervous clearing of throats. The watchers chafe uncomfortably in their funeral clothes. They wash the feelings away with endless cups of weak coffee. Sam's empty chair at the table is a silent reproach.

"If only he coulda hung on just a bit longer," Ernie adds. "It's always hard to wait it out this time of year. If only he coulda held out till…"

"He shoulda said something," Paul interrupts. "He shoulda told us if his nerves were bad. He didn't have to go that way. Summer is just around the corner."

But summer is just a vague memory for some of us. In January, time stands still. The smoke from the wood burning stoves curls lazily into the air, ice shacks dot the bay and bodies hunger for light. We watch for the desolate days to lengthen, for the depressing darkness to end.

As watchers we use each other as buffers against the merciless monotony of winter in the Cove. Some of us find solace in the sameness of each day. For Sam, I now believe it was a slow torture.

I can only say these things in remembrance, of course. My image of the watchers is shifting. Now I see men who are still vital, who can still make a contribution, wasting away in the limbo of premature retirement. These men had been independent, productive and appreciated. Now they must manufacture ways to feed the pride that once came from being in charge. We are sidelined from the game; we watch and wait.

Except Sam. He didn't want to be part of the ritual any more. He could no longer look forward to the changing of the seasons or the changing of the guard.

In July, Janet Cove is a paradise on Earth. The tourists

from "down south" come in their fine cars and their designer jeans. The American yachts glide into port, rubbing our noses in their affluence and their arrogance. The transient strangers represent the reality of a globe divided into the haves and have nots.

Yet, the watchers are in their glory then. The adrenaline is pumping as they go about the serious business of patrolling their turf.

As for me, I am often near the harbour taking my pictures. My camera lens serves as my window on the world, my way of making sense of it all.

I see Ernie and Walter stirring after a winter of confinement. They are back on the job. They drive their cars to the waterfront and each man takes charge of a station. Someone stakes out the elevated parking lot above the shower houses near the docks. From here, this unofficial harbour master can note how many boats have been rented out by the charter company. He can also oversee the grassy area where the boaters walk their dogs and foul the picnic area.

Farther along the shore, there's a spreading willow tree that provides a perfect vantage point for another watcher. Through binoculars, he gets a bird's eye view of the skimpy swim wear, the co-ordinated jogging suits and the fake salon tans. The yacht owners are at once objects of fierce animosity and endless fascination. On a calm summer evening, he hears the tinkling of ice in tall glasses, the popping of champagne corks and the rippling of laughter from dockside parties.

For a few glorious moments, the watcher dreams. He embarks on an imaginary voyage to tropical climes, to the playgrounds of the idle rich. For an instant he is transported beyond the narrow harbour of Janet Cove and into an ocean of possibilities.

Like old soldiers re-enacting the War of 1812, the watchers monitor the Yankee invaders in their port-of-call. Shift change is a solemn military drill. One of the watchers will pull his pick-up truck alongside the waiting car under the willow tree. With windows rolled down, and sleeves rolled up, they exchange vital counter-intelligence information.

After a few minutes of updating the weather forecast, the catch of the day and the size of the masts, one vehicle slowly pulls away. Like retired undercover cops who can't quite give up the excitement of the stake-out, the watchers finish their appointed rounds.

In the evening, the sentinels salute the setting sun and scan the running lights visible on tardy sailboats. Sometimes a watcher will complete one last patrol of the private campground just up the shoreline. A head count of the campers helps to round out the surveillance report next morning at coffee. After the de-briefing, the town rumour mill has plenty of new data to process.

Yes, if I can make it to July, I will be in the clear. When the fish are biting, the sails billowing and the white caps dancing, the watchers have a mission. We set up a schedule that restores order and self-importance. Even if the world has no more use for us, we are judges, superintendents, overseers, captains and inspectors in our summer fantasies.

I take my place at the lookout on the escarpment. I snap my pictures. I try to frame my world in the best possible light.

I don't think Sam could keep up the pretense. Maybe he could never truly be a watcher. Sam was a doer. He had to be in the mainstream, in control. He couldn't be guarding the home fires; he had to be on the firing line. For him, passive contemplation and self-deception were intolerable.

I find myself speculating about Sam more and more as

the last stretch of January arrives. I can't stop wondering about his last hours, about what finally drove him to pull the trigger. As always, I am afraid to reveal my feelings to the others. They will dismiss me and despise me, as they do all men who think too deeply. I do not risk their ridicule. I watch and wait with them. And all the while it gnaws at me. Could I have helped Sam? Did I watch him go under, while I remained the clinical observer?

I am beginning to lose it. My perspective, I mean. It no longer works to take my camera and to freeze frame the landscape. I look to the faces of the old men for answers. The watchers pull the circle tighter and huddle in suspended animation till spring.

I find myself coming later and later to coffee. I am a bit more quiet than usual. Nobody tries to draw me out of my silence; it's none of their business. In Janet Cove, we mostly mind our own business.

Visitation

Natalie Wilson

No music plays at this funeral. That's what Mary thinks of: Johnny Cash singing *Ring of Fire*, Daddy humming along, sitting at the kitchen table, bottle of beer fingered by one hand, him holding a cigarette, holding the rest of his body upright, somehow. Daddy could always pass out and never tip from his kitchen chair. The song won't leave Mary's mind, keeps circling. She wishes they had the record at home, that she could plunk it on the turntable, turn it up, make the head echoes go. The song has been inside for two days now.

Mama is tired. Lines have sunk the sockets of her eyes, anchoring them open. She stands. Talks to people. Gives these small smiles, acknowledgements to the people who work here, as they get ready to usher the visitors through the door. Her shoulder blades poke like clothespins on a line. She hasn't slept much this week.

Mary is sitting. She is the only one sitting, though couches rim the dripping carpet and brass of this room. Thick, comfortable sofas. Everyone is important, this furniture says. Boxes of tissue everywhere, behind lamps, under silk plants, behind tasteful silk greenery. Mary wears a navy blue corduroy jumper that hangs nearly to her ankles. It is a lousy late-April day of rain mixed with snow.

It is the beginning, the obligatory being here to comfort those who come to comfort them. The first evening of public mourning. Tomorrow is the real service, though to Mary it began two days ago, when Daddy died. The casket is closed, but Mary still sees him, scarecrow stick with mouth and eyes wide open, mummy thin, skin fallen back, finally dead. The body in there isn't Daddy, anymore: even with the nicotine stains on his fingers, the clothes that the funeral people have dressed him in.

Candace is pregnant. Mary is going to be an aunt. Auntie. Thus the stress, the tears, the worn outness of Candace the last two months. She has waited until now, to be sure, before telling anyone. Jacob tells Mary as they are waiting for Mama in the pickup. His voice is dull, a butter knife. He cannot grasp it. What a baby means. It means they will not travel. It means they will not leave now, for Australia, or for anywhere. Their passports are still in their envelopes, tucked in a kitchen drawer. Mama is going to be a grandmama. Mary will be an aunt.

The news makes Mary vaguely sad, more jealous. Candace is twenty-four. Mary is closer and closer to thirty. It isn't fair, that Jacob gets things first. A wife. A job. A baby. Mary doesn't say this, and Jacob tells her Candace does not want anyone to know, yet. Not Mary or Mama. Candace doesn't want the attention, right now. He grips the steering wheel with white knuckles against his cold red skin. Jacob tells Mary that Candace can't seem to stop crying, some days. That she's been crying a lot, lately.

Trumpet blast. I'm falling, falling, falling. Ring of Fire. God, how Daddy loved Johnny Cash. The Man in Black. Like the shadow Mary saw that night in the parking lot, cigarette ember burning, cowboy boots. Ring of Fire.

"Hormones," Mary says. As if she knows. Reassurance. She watches as Mama picks her way in her dress shoes and spring coat toward the pickup. They are on their way to the funeral parlour. "It's a big change in a woman's body. She'll be okay."

The trumpets, or whatever they are, suck her back into the song. Brassy blasts make it impossible for Mary to stamp the tune from her mind. She can't remember all of the words, and she ends up returning to what she does know, over and over again.

Marty is here. Mary sees his familiar form appear in the doorway, move toward Jacob and Candace, look over and smile at Mary. She smiles back, she thinks. Her mind is disconnected, no longer in service. She is having difficulty switching it back. She tries again to shake the music from her head. Fails.

She would like to close her eyes, forget this place. Go home and cry, though she doesn't know what for. Mary hasn't cried much now that Daddy is no longer living. The part of her that loves Daddy is entirely empty. What difference does it make, now?

"How are you doing, pumpkin?" Mama sinks into the cushion beside Mary, has left her post by the door to come and speak words that Daddy said to Mary hundreds of thousands of times. Never once has Mama ever called Mary pumpkin. Just Daddy. Just once. Now.

Mama is wearing a long blue denim skirt and a navy blue blazer, a soft pink blouse underneath. She looks beautiful, though the grey is peeking through the roots of her blond hair, though her almost perfectly made-up eyes are swollen, though her hands still shake, just a bit. Nicotine withdrawal. Mary knows even she would smoke cigarette after cigarette right now, if she could. Mama has not smoked since the day before yesterday, at eleven thirteen in the morning. One-one-one-three on the glow red digital in Daddy's room, bright enough for them to record medication by. Mary wonders if that moment is engraved in Mama's mind, too: Mary opening the back door, full of surprise, full of wonder, with words. *Mama, I think Daddy just died. I don't think he's breathing anymore. Can you come and check?*

Ten minutes before seven. Soon, strangers will start arriving. Not strangers, but people Mary doesn't know, doesn't really want to see. People who will say things like we're so sorry and how are you doing and we haven't seen you since you were a little girl. People Mary won't care if she remembers.

"I want you to come with me." Mama puts out a hand, wraps it firm around Mary's sitting in her lap, then squeezes, hard. She turns so that her eyes look straight into Mary's. "Come help me, lovie," she whispers. "Okay?"

Mama's words burst the chorus blaring in Mary's mind.

"Okay," Mary answers, numb from the sudden silence in her head. And she stands with Mama, begins to walk toward the inside right corner by the door.

As they move, Corrina comes. She is wearing black pants and a long sweater of swirling colours, deep greens and purples and oranges and reds. Her hair is longer than Mary remembers, open and flowing down her back. Eyes wide, calm and serious, Corrina just appears, sees Jacob first and moves there, magic across the floor. She hugs him once, meets Candace with a small smile, and then puts one hand out to Marty, says something with a bigger smile, shakes his hand.

Then they wrap their arms around one another, stand and hold on like sisters, like lovers. Mary smells the smooth softness of Corry's hair, feels the bones beneath her sweater, bends into her friend's shoulder and begins to cry. Corrina just stands, hugs her tighter, pulls her close with one hand on Mary's head, like she is holding a baby, a small animal, a treasure of sorts. It is all Mary can do not to let her knees give out beneath her. It is a gift, this. To just cry. To just stand. Her friend is here. Has come for her.

When Mrs. Beaucage opens the front door, Mary thinks her heart is going to fly out of her mouth because it is beating so fast. The plastic handles on the shopping bag she is carrying are biting into her fingers, sinking big red marks into her skin. Mrs. Beaucage is tall and thin, long hair pulled back with a tie at the back of her neck, with a cigarette in one hand. Somehow Mary says it: "Can your little girl come out and play?"

Corrina is so pretty. That's all Mary can think about as they wander into Corrina's back yard, settle the bag of playthings that Mary has brought with her on the patio stones, shuffle down to size one another up. She is so pretty with all of that hair and those beautiful eyes.

"Thanks," Corrina says, looking at her sort of weirdly.

Mary realizes she spoke that last thought out loud. She does things like that sometimes, without thinking. Sometimes she forgets what she is imagining and what is real. She gets in trouble at school some days for staring out the window too long. There's no magic mirror out there, Sister Mary Helen will say. Now back to your work. The whole class is going to be finished, and you won't even have the first page done.

"Where did you live before here?" Mary is trying to think of things to ask that don't sound nosy. Mama says Mary asks nosy questions, and that she should mind her business.

"Just outside of town. On the reserve there." Corrina stares at Mary for a short time, looks at her snug shorts and dirty t-shirt. "Have you been there before?"

"No." Mary is puzzled. Do people live outside of towns?

Does that mean in the country? But what is a reserve? Isn't that what Nanny makes with strawberries every summer?

"It's a place where Indians live," Corrina explains. She puts one finger to her chest, points at herself. "I'm an Indian. So are my mom and dad. And my grandparents. We all used to live out there, together. But my mom and dad wanted to move in to town, to live here for a while."

"You're lucky." It's all Mary can think of to say, and she really means it. "I wish I lived with my Nanny and Poppy. My Nanny makes gumdrop cake for me, whenever she visits. We only get to see her at Christmas and in the summer, and sometimes when they drive here for a visit, after school starts. It would be great, to have them here all the time."

Corrina just looks at Mary, sort of turns her head to one side. Then she just shrugs, and smiles. Mary can't believe how beautiful she is. All of that hair....

"Do you want to play detective?" Mary asks, reaching for her bag.

"Thanks," is all Mary can manage, surprised to see Corrina's tears when she finally pulls away, straightens her own shoulders, uses a balled up Kleenex in one of her fists to soak the wet from her eyes. Mary figures she already must look like hell. At not even seven-fifteen.

"When did you come home?" Mary suddenly longs to talk about normal things, about everyday stuff, about life other than the one she has been living for the last five months. She needs to feel almost adult, at least for a few minutes, again.

"Earlier today. I went to my parents' place on the reserve, and drove in from there." Corrina's voice has not changed, but it has always sounded different on the phone. Not quite real enough. Not quite Corrina. Mary can't believe that it has only been two days since their last phone call.

"How's school?" Mary wants to hear about Corrina's life, wants to hear what it is like, in Toronto, where Mary would never have the nerve to go. She wants to hear about the places Corry sees, about whether or not she's met a new man, a nice man, a man who doesn't drink too much or do cocaine or fool around with other women. Or with other men. Mary wishes, just for a second, that she could have such a life. A life of exciting possibilities. A life away from this town.

"It's fine. Busy." Corry just shrugs, manages a little smile. The tears are drying on her face, little disappearing pools of wet in the corner of each dark eye. Then she speaks again. "I phoned Marsha in London. To tell her. I thought she might want to know when the funeral was, and I didn't know if you had the time to reach her. So I gave her a call. I hope you don't mind."

"No, I don't mind." Mary is surprised. She hasn't thought of Marsha for months, years, generations. "She probably won't be able to come, though. London's pretty far. Especially with three kids."

"She said she's coming." Corrina's voice is as surprised as Mary's. "She said she'll bring the kids and let them stay with her mom." Corrina shrugs, the tiny movement Mary has seen a hundred thousand times before. It brings Mary back to high school, to listening to Corry tell her not to worry about it, to not get so uptight, to relax, to let it go.

When Mary and Ray finally break up, Corrina and Mary spend a full weekend listening to "Love Hurts" by Nazareth on the stereo, over and over again. When Mary tells Ray that maybe they shouldn't see one another any more, Ray goes and kicks in one of the giant mirrored windows at one of the banks downtown. He gets arrested, and then phones Mary later that night crying, telling her that he loves her. Corry sits beside Mary the whole conversation, and shakes her head no when Ray asks Mary if he can come over, can come and talk to her, see her. The two of them spend the first night at Mary's house and the second at Corry's, so that their parents won't keep telling them to turn down the music. They smoke three joints in the crawl space off Corrina's basement. Corrina lets Mary talk and talk, all weekend. And never says one bad thing about Ray.

"I've missed you." They never really talk this way. Their friendship begins always where it's left off, whether it's been weeks, months, years. It doesn't matter what either of them has done, has seen, has failed at. But now Mary feels they've missed out on something, by not speaking those words before.

"I know," Corrina says, then smiles the smile they'd share as co-conspirators in junior high school. "I wish we could find a way to keep all of our lives together, even when we live apart. You haven't told me anything about you and Marty. I want the dirt! A younger man! The boy next door! Well, next door to my house, anyway. I can't believe it! I want to know what's been going on."

Mary forgets where she is, what she is doing, and laughs. Really laughs, though not long. It is like her eyes open, her tears dry, for just long enough. So simple. A caption on a Snoopy cartoon. So right.

Mary holds Corrina's hand. Feels the cool smoothness of her friend's long fingers against the sweaty wet of her own. She squeezes Corry's hand once before letting go.

"Thanks for coming, Corry." She is uncomfortable again, aware of where she is. At the beginning of her father's funeral. Her Daddy's death. Alliteration. Though at least for now the song has gone.

Corrina stares back at her, with that way of opening her eyes wider, making her face look straighter, her cheekbones sleeker, when she wants to. She keeps her voice casual. "You know, Mary, that there was no question about me not being here." And then she floats, back to Jacob, to Candace and Marty, stopping once to wrap her slender arms around Mama's neck.

Mary stands, tries to listen to the awkward conversations of people from church, from the men who worked for years with Daddy, from the folks who drank with him at the Rock 'n' Tap, from the old friends from high school, from when Daddy used to curl, play hockey. Mary gives up trying to remember names, and begins to count. All of these people, but not one visited Daddy when he was living. Not one came to the house, though some people telephoned. Not one told Daddy that they were sorry, that this was happening to him. Not a soul. And now that he's dead, they're all here. Amazing.

"Do you really care that he's dead?" Mary knows what reaction she would get if she asked the question aloud. She wants to scream it. Will they think of him again, in a week, two weeks, tomorrow, next year? Will they remember Gary Randall when the bulbs are all in bloom and spring is finally here, after this dreadful winter? Will they remember him as a terrific card player, a pool shark, a guy who tries to help people, even though sometimes he's too drunk to do it? Will they remember that he is a Daddy of two, and in a number of months would be a Granddaddy? What will they remember? What will Mary remember?

Mary is worn by seven forty-five. She wants to sit again, to fold into herself and rest. How can Mama look so composed, so solid, while being so battered and tired? Though Mary is beginning now to understand, to see that Mama is relieved. Mama is thankful that Daddy has died. The cancer terrified her. His suffering terrified her. Daddy being alive like that was Mama's worst nightmare. His death released her.

God, there is still almost an hour more, still more tick tock minutes to endure as the daughter of the dead one, the daughter of the widow, the lost child. Mary wants nothing more than to sink into bed, to take off these shoes and silly dress and to scrub her face and brush her teeth and cry. But she also wants Marty to lie beside her and kiss her skin softly all over. She wants him to run his fingers over the dips and rolls that make up the round of her belly, the spread of her thighs. She misses sleeping with Marty, misses their apartment, misses their bed, their Friday nights in front of the TV, wants to be with him now.

"How do you feel about being a Daddy?" It's what Mary really wants to ask Jacob as he stands, concentrating on the plush carpet, denting tiny rings in it with the toe of his patent dress shoe, holding on to one of Candace's hands. But Mary can't ask him that yet, here, in this place, with Marty and Corrina and Candace close by, because it is still a secret, is still not knowledge, yet. Mary will tell Marty later. Tonight. She will ask Marty to come stay at the house again; she will take him to her room with her, so that she can hold him, just for a little while. Warm her bones.

When Mary looks up again Mama is there, speaking. Gord Carswell stands beside her, a sort of smile on his face, his hands placed carefully at his sides. All of Gord's height is in his legs. The man from church. His waist almost fits at Mama's elbow.

Mama has pulled herself together, again. Has stitched the tears back up. Mary can't help but study the two of them, and wonder. This is a strong friendship. This is a church friendship. Do they love one another? Lusty love? Have they ever made love? Will Gord take care of Mama, now that Daddy is gone? What do they talk about, when they're alone? Have they asked for God's forgiveness? For God's blessing? God. Who will stay with Mama now, in that big house, still full of cancer? Who will go out with her for dinner, on Friday nights? What will Mama do, now? "Mary, Jacob. Candace. My thoughts are with you. This is a sad and difficult time. You're all in my prayers." Right. He's a deacon, Mary thinks. A man who warms the soul. But what about body, fingers, lips, toes? Will he keep Mama warm?

Mary misses the introductions, but pastes on a smile. She has an excuse: she has met Gord before. Corrina even reaches over and shakes Gord's hand. Mary remembers how she told Corrina her suspicions, all those nights ago in Iroquois Falls, somewhere in another time. Mary thinks of the fun of that weekend. Their lives were all so different, then. Mary didn't know Gord's name, yet. But Corrina knows who he is, from Mama, from her tears.

"Jacob, Gord has offered us his van for tomorrow. So that we can all come to the funeral home together, instead of in two trips. He'll leave keys with you tonight, will park it in the visitor's area at your building, and then I'll drive him home. He can walk here tomorrow morning and pick it up, because we'll go in the limousine to the church and cemetery."

When will this evening end? All Mary can think about now is going home, even to the home that is empty now of Daddy, even though Daddy stays here and they don't, even though Daddy is left alone. Mary is without her Daddy. Without the man her children would call Poppy, if she has them. Marty's niece and nephew call his dad Grandpapa. It's a long word for little ones, one that reminds Mary of a polka. There won't be a Poppy for Jacob's child. Daddy has died. He has died. He is dead.

The lump in her throat is too big. The burning in her eyes too intense. Mary can't do it, anymore. Can't stand. Can't see. Can't speak. Can't listen. That's it, that's all. It's all she can think. The words swirl, whirl, begin to dance, pop and dazzle in the corners of her mind.

And the Man in Black steps in. He's a shadow in the corner of Mary's eye. With one wave of his hand, the song starts. Trumpets, please. Flames, please.

Marty. He takes Mary's arm, holds it near the flabby part, the upper part. The soft part. Circles his fingers around it. Softly. "We're going to get a coffee downstairs." He doesn't look at Mary. "We'll be back in a few minutes."

Her own movement breaks the cycle. The song. The pounding of her heart somewhere inside her head. "Thank you," she says. "Thanks." She concentrates on holding the railing, on pushing each foot down one stair.

"Hey, it's okay," is Marty's answer. He waits patiently as she puts one foot after the other, like the movement is new for her. His hand is warm. "You'll be okay."

STILL LIFE WITH FEET

Susan Eldridge-Vautour

This evening, the sun casts shadows like spells. It is late summer and six people sit spread across the grass along the riverbank. The sun lies down with the water in the river's bed. The reflected intensity of their embrace saturates the scene. Everyone and everything seems lit from within. Reeds and tall grasses sit still, long and languid, allowing themselves to be stroked with pure colour. Their bright citric green licks across the rich chocolate brown river below them.

"It almost doesn't even look *real*," Charlotte gasps as she runs for her camera, almost stepping on Elaine's fingers in the process. "Sorry hon. Okay?" Charlotte apologizes, then bolts to her car without waiting for a response.

She snatches up her old camera, appreciating its heft as she lifts it out the open window. She doesn't understand people's preference for the small, light digital cameras that are so popular now. They don't even make that satisfying click and wind noise. Just point and shoot. Her camera is a hand me down from an old boyfriend who has moved on to digital and keeps all his photos 'virtually', on computer. Tommy doesn't even call them photographs anymore. He refers now to 'j-pegs' and 'bitmaps', embracing the terminology along with the technology. Charlotte is new to photography. She is only beginning to remember to capture moments as she is living them. Good light, she thinks, is as fleeting as happiness. You have to notice it. When beauty unfolds, Charlotte wants snap it up. Each photo, to her, is like a butterfly; a winged and fluttering moment, caught and pressed onto a page for her to look at anytime. Mike teases her, lately, about the steadily increasing number of albums she is filling up. Really, though, he is thrilled with the 'development' of her new hobby. He always says this to her and to their friends, eyebrows raised, enjoying the pun, "...get it? Development?" Mike enjoys the groans each time.

Charlotte returns to the river where the others have closed the gap left by her absence. As she slips past them, she sees them smiling and talking and sipping from their glasses of Sally's homemade wine. Charlotte makes a mental note to take a few photographs of these, her dearest friends, while there is still light enough.

In no time, she has cranked off a dozen frames: several of the reeds and grass, the path of yellow light traced by the sun across the water's surface, the gnarled tree roots breaking through the water, a tiny green frog on a perfectly heart-shaped lily pad, the deserted dock, floating with Sally's children's footprints remaining puddled and now alight with reflected sunset. Charlotte regrets not having taken a few shots of the kids themselves. They looked like river elves as they emerged from the water, glistening. She is certain that the footprint image will be the strongest. She actually knows this just as she's clicked the shutter. There is a quality of composition as well as a hint of magic. Visually, it embodies the surreal quality of the evening light that had first propelled her to retrieve her camera. Part of the creative process for Charlotte is naming each shot. By attaching words to them, she is able to decipher the language of the images she is drawn to, a translation. As she selects a spot in the circle, she is still contemplating what the footprint portrait says. She knows that Michael will appreciate that particular photo. He is bewildered by her choice of subject matter sometimes. Particularly, he is amused by her small collection of foot shots. Her current favourite is one she took in Sally's kitchen, the terracotta tiles providing the backdrop for two pairs of feet. Ginger's sweet 12-year-old feet are bare with her toe nails painted black and a beaded hemp anklet dangling loosely. The feet are on tip toe. Elaine's black-leather-motorcycle-boot clad feet face them. One boot is resting on a chunky heel. The other is on its toe. It is obvious from this unusual perspective that the girls are kitchen dancing (a sort of tradition at Sally's). *Reckless.* Anyway, Michael is bound to be entertained that she is now including *ghosts* of feet in her collection.

Sally shifts over, patting the blanket beside her. Michael has refilled her glass and it has passed from hand to hand to hand until it has reached her, more or less intact. Elaine has pointedly taken a sip as a hint to Michael that her glass, too, is empty. Also, a bit has sloshed out on its final journey from Wry's hand to Char's.

"Oopsie-Daisy" he says, making everyone giggle.

"*Oopsie-Daisy?!*" Mike teases.

"Grace strikes again" says Wry, wryly, speaking of his mother, dead a year and who was of a certain age and whose dated sayings had a way of finding their way out of Wry's beautifully formed lips. Wry's 'real' name is Wright but his friends call him Wry or sometimes Rye if he's enjoying one of his rare nights imbibing whiskey on ice. Wry could be a male model. He is *that* good-looking. What he actually does for a living is far less glamorous. He works at a halfway house for alcoholics and drug users. He serves a lot of coffee, listens to a lot of sad stories and cleans up vomit "and worse" he says ominously, leaving it at that. Wry is having some difficulty dealing with Grace's death. They were very close. Grace had Wry late in life. A postscript. She loved Wry the best because she had the luxury of time and patience. With her older children, she had been at her busiest—working at the library, raising three girls and attempting to live up to the social expectations of the time. Her house was impeccably clean, her girls well dressed and polite, her husband pampered. By the time she had Wright, the girls were off to college, she was down to part time hours at the library and women's liberation had set in all around her. Grace took to the women's movement like a 'duck to water'. She became less of a slave to her house and demanded sweetly that Charles take on his share of the household responsibilities. Charles did as he was asked. Truth be told, Grace still pampered Charles but she did so because she chose to. So it was that Wry grew up with an abundance of attention in a happy, if comfortably dishevelled home.

Tonight, Wry has brought Brett, who is relatively new to the circle but who is well-liked. He is an Aussie who works as a bartender at the local gay bar where he makes outrageous tips, primarily due to his accent that he emphasizes at work. In reality, he's been in Canada for over 15 years and his accent has all but disappeared. Wry and Brett joke about the irony of their respective professions all the time. Wet Nurse and Dry Doc.

Michael and Wry have known each other forever. That is since high school. They attended in the same small town and found in each other someone to drink with and talk to. They found themselves outside the mainstream crowd of rowdy young men who thought the only topics of conversation were sports and motors and girls. Neither Mike nor Wry had found these conversations interesting. Of course, these days, the good old boys from their hometown could easily pin Wry's early lack of interest in 'manly' pursuits to his homosexuality. The fact is, Wry could almost certainly kick any of their 'redneck-asses'. At 35 he is in excellent physical shape while most of their former classmates are bloated with bad diets, beer and smoking. Michael, for his part, was perfectly capable of pulling a motor apart, fixing what was wrong and reassembling it. He just didn't feel the need to discuss it. As for girls, even in high school, he preferred *women* and he also didn't feel the need to discuss *that*. So Mike and Wry had fallen into a friendship that had lasted a couple of decades, through one failed, brief marriage for Michael and through Wry's big step 'out of the closet'.

Charlotte points to the drop of spilled red wine on her wrist which Wry quickly slurps up making her giggle and pull her arm away.

"*Hey*, I thought I never had to worry about the best friend-wife scenario!" Mike jokes.

"Don't worry, hon, he's just a lush. It's the alcohol he's after." Charlotte ruffles Wry's hair and gives him a gentle shove.

As Wry lands in Brett's lap, Charlotte snaps a photograph. They look like tousle-haired boys, wild and innocent.

Charlotte looks across the circle to see Sally and Elaine sharing a quiet toast. Their eyes are soft and their smiles lift them beyond mortal beauty. They are suddenly two angels, holding hands, wings touching.

Charlotte reaches for the camera again and gets one lovely shot before the holy pair turn in an instant into silly school girls, tongues sticking out and eyes crossed. That is a problem. In trying to hold onto a moment you sometimes destroy it. Still the self-consciousness only lasts a few seconds before everyone regains their relaxed composure.

Everyone is making an effort to get used to Charlotte's new weapon. Mike is not the only one pleased with her new love of photography. It is the happiest anyone has seen her in months. Char's depression is not clinical. That is, she's never been diagnosed. Her friends know, however, that she's been struggling for some time. They know about her frequent headaches and fatigue. She hasn't mentioned to any of them the worrisome memory loss (which is partly why she's taken up photography, hoping to hold onto her life in 4x6 glossy bits). Overall, Charlotte's friends feel they are being rewarded with her regained enthusiasm as well as some remarkable portraits of themselves and each other. Even Elaine, who never has thought of herself as attractive, enjoys the shots Charlotte has taken of her. Within their circle, Charlotte has taken on the unofficial position of chronicler.

Elaine and Charlotte have been friends since high school, too. They met in their graduating year when Elaine's family moved out of the big city mainly because they were worried about their teenage daughter running with the wrong crowd. Elaine and Charlotte hit it off right away. They spent the next few years in one another's presence throughout various romances for each of them. Charlotte met Michael at college and while Elaine missed having her to herself, she was happy for her and liked Mike well enough. When Elaine went to Alaska for a summer she fell in love for the first time. None of the boyfriends she'd had really made her feel any of those powerful things she kept hearing about. No butterflies, no tingling, no panic filled need. Then she met Dusty. Dusty was a dancer in one of the 'saloons'. Wild red hair and soft blue eyes. Friday and Saturday nights Dusty would put on layers of lace and satin and kick up her sexy heels on stage. Elaine was sitting at the bar enjoying her third cold beer and laughing at the antics of a very silly man seated next to her when she saw Dusty. Dusty swished by and then turned and winked at Elaine.

"Hey, I think she likes you," buddy noted sarcastically. Elaine turned several shades of pink and found herself speechless.

She glanced toward the stage, trying to see Dusty without turning her head. Her cheeks felt flushed and her stomach was turning. It was like nausea but not so unpleasant. When the set was finished Elaine could not believe it when Dusty tapped buddy on the shoulder and asked "Mind if I cut in?"

The baffled man shook his head and offered his bar stool with a gallant sweep of his arm. "Well, *I* sure ain't getting anywhere. Good luck."

The romance was vivid but it turned out that Dusty's intensity was not to be contained within the boundaries of a relationship. Elaine's heart was broken but full when she returned from Alaska. Charlotte listened as Elaine poured out seven songs, lyrics and music, within her first week home. She actually recorded these '7 Dusty Tunes' onto a cd which launched a moderately successful music career for Elaine. Dusty still sends quirky postcards to Elaine from all over the world.

Elaine now lives with Sally and Sally's children in Sally's big, rambling house in the country. Elaine travels quite a bit, touring with her band, but loves having a home to come to. Charlotte is happy for Elaine and only a little jealous of the closeness of the girls' relationship. The kids seem to like Elaine, although they don't call her 'mom'.

Elaine doesn't see herself as a maternal being. She does, however, treat everyone with a remarkable amount of respect, including the kids. Heath is 17 and remembers his father better than his younger sister can. He can't recall the man showing anyone much respect. Heath has found it easier to relate to Elaine over the past few years than to his mom. Sally often treats him like a child. Elaine is just there, easy to be with. He feels lucky. Elaine has been a sort of ally, reminding his mom to give him some space to figure things out for himself. Elaine is reasonable where his mom is emotional. Besides, even though Elaine's music is not exactly his style, it's still cool that she goes off on tour with a band and has cd's and fans. Sometimes, he's allowed to go and sit at a table selling disks and t-shirts to a crowd of mostly lesbian women and listen to Elaine perform. Elaine taught him to play and bought him his first guitar.

Ginger is 12 and can't remember her father at all. Sally left him a few months after Ginger was born. Sally and Elaine met shortly afterward. Ginger calls Elaine 'Wayne'. When Ginger was small, she had a speech impediment while she was learning to label all the things in her world. When she started school she attended speech sessions where she learned to get her throat and tongue properly involved in the communication process. Elaine, however, remained 'Wayne' and Elaine doesn't mind a bit. In a way, she enjoys the boyishness of the name. In turn, Elaine calls the girl Gingersnap and always snaps her fingers when she speaks the name. A single snap of her long fingers and a smile on her lips as if the name in her mouth is actually something sweet and tasty. Ginger knows she is well loved by both of the women in her home. It's ironic, Charlotte thinks, Elaine has children while she, herself, does not. Not for lack of trying. Charlotte regrets not having had a child when she had the chance. Sometimes one chance is all that's offered.

Charlotte is thinking about her girl friend's family as she returns her camera to the car where it will be safe from the impending spill of drinks as the darkness closes in on the group at the river. The sun has completely set leaving only a faint glow above the western tree line, not really enough light for photographs anyway.

As she reaches in through the window a blinding pain spreads out from the base of her skull. She feels her fingers and toes tingle and go numb. The camera falls onto the passenger seat and she falls backwards, landing hard on the ground. Charlotte initially thinks she'll end up with some nasty bruises, but soon knows that she's in serious trouble when she can neither feel nor move her body. It's like those times that she's had near misses driving. The world spinning slowly in front of her windshield as she waits to see what will happen next, knowing she has lost control. Charlotte feels warmth flooding inside her head. For a moment she argues with herself, knowing that the brain has no feeling; not knowing how she knows this, she guesses she's read it somewhere. But then she thinks of all the pulsing headaches she's had over the years and knows there is feeling somewhere in the cranium if not in the brain itself. The pain is replaced by dullness and then by darkness lit with memories dissolving into one another.

...gilded strands of green curving towards the edge of the world... *Chocolate Margarita*. ...tommy, the moment she falls succinctly out of love with him ... inside his red sports car outside the abortion clinic ... a basket with champagne and flowers in the back seat ... his face, crestfallen that his celebration has fallen flat as day old bubbly ... *Burst Bubbles*. ...elaine's freckled face, wearing a smile deep and warm as a cup of tea ..."Cuppa?" as she pours a steaming brew into a misshapen mug—the first Charlotte has ever thrown

... elaine knowing when tea is necessary, already adding the perfect amount of honey ... *Bittersweet.* ...michael, his eyes wet with laughter as he enjoys one of her stories of one of her days ... she feels comforted by the embrace of his gaze ... has fallen in love with him upon waking from their first night together ... his arms loosely but securely around her ... her first thought that morning is *Welcome Home.* ...wry, hovering over grace's hospital bed, his hand resting over hers lightly ... not knowing charlotte has entered the room as he sings a verse from an old war time tune into grace's ear ... the first time charlotte realizes he has an absolutely beautiful voice ... *Lullabye.* ...sally and elaine holding hands ... *Sugar and Spice.* ...wry and brett tumbling across the grass ...*Snips and Snails (of course).* ... heath and ginger spraying river water from their copper heads ... *Amber Drizzle.* ... water colour footprints ... a plum sky in a pool left by dripping children's feet ... phantoms ... rorschach inkblot butterfly wings ... charlotte trying to hold this picture in her mind but the outline evaporating ... ... *Flight with Wings Still Wet.*

Mike and Elaine stand at the photo counter while the others are gathering food and wine. Provisions. They have all been steeping together in grief at Sally's big, ramshackle home for a week now. Charlotte is everywhere and nowhere. She has taken so many photographs and they hang from walls, sit on shelves and hide in albums. Mike wishes that he had taken more pictures of Charlotte. Her letters are strewn through boxes and drawers. Elaine knows there will be booby traps for years to come, Charlotte moments waiting to happen. Mike hasn't even been able to go home yet because the house is absolutely full of her. Her clothes, her scent, her mess, her music, her books— everything except her self. Everyone is meant to come over tonight to help him settle in. They'll cook a big dinner, listen to music, and drink too much. It's the finale. Elaine has written a song. Some of them are expected to turn up at work on Monday. The allotted grieving period is drawing to a close.

Mike is startled when Elaine speaks in her whiskey voice, "If every picture tells a story, there's a library there." Elaine waves toward the files of photos the clerk is casually flipping through. "Life stories in glossy purple envelopes." Michael thinks, suddenly, that the clerk should perhaps be more reverential in her handling of them. He takes the package she hands him and they go out to sit in the car to wait for the others. Elaine watches him as he doesn't open it. His thumbs are rubbing across its glossy surface.

"Now? Or later, with the others?" Elaine asks. Michael notices how pale Elaine is. Her freckles even seem faded, her eyes clouded. There are lines between her eyebrows. He gathers her into his arms and they hold on tightly to each other. It occurs to Michael that Elaine is hurting just as much as he is and he realizes that he is relieved to not be alone in his sorrow.

"It's like I'm starving for these crumbs," Elaine says, touching the envelope.

The first photo is a surprise. It wasn't taken the evening of the party, the evening that Charlotte died. It was taken on a sunny morning a week or so earlier. Mike remembers he had been drinking coffee in the garden and looking at the blooms on the oregano and inhaling its fragrance when he heard a noise. He turned to find Charlotte practically on top of him, the camera inches from his face. "That should be a *fabulous* shot, a close up of my nostrils!" Instead it *was* a fabulous shot ... of Charlotte. Her reflection caught in the sunglasses he had been wearing. Her hair is messy from sleep and she's wearing her long raggy t-shirt. Only half of her face is visible behind the camera but her happiness is clear.

"Look for your reflection only in clear forest pools and in the eyes of someone who loves you," Elaine says quietly, "and you will always be beautiful. Charlotte knew *that* well enough."

"That's why we all look good in her portraits; she loved us," Mike observes as they study the rest of the photos.

The last is the one of footprints. It *is* a striking image. Mike remembers seeing Charlotte down at the dock taking what must have been this photo. He saw her take the picture then continue to look through the view finder for a moment longer. He had noticed the contemplative look on her face as she came up from the river. Mike remembers the feel of her long, cotton skirt that brushed over his hand, her scent as she breezed by him, and the half smile she tossed over her shoulder to him as she crossed the yard to the car.

Mike begins to laugh. "She was haunted by goddamn *feet*."

Elaine sees his eyes crinkle at their outer corners while their inner corners are leaking more tears. She wraps her arm around Mike's shoulders. "Charlotte is reminding us to enjoy the moments, they're passing quickly."

Mike and Elaine are still holding onto each other when Wry returns to the car. He sets his brown paper liquor store bags on the back seat.

"You guys doing okay?" he asks as he climbs into the car and slides onto Elaine's lap. He kisses Elaine on the cheek, then leans over and hugs Mike. "I love you guys, you know."

"We know, we know, now get off me." Elaine is shoving him out of the car.

"You incorrigible flirt!" scolds Sally as she arrives at the car. "Leave my woman alone!"

"I just left him for a moment ..." Brett dramatically apologizes to Sally for the bad behaviour of his boyfriend. Sally and Brett pile the grocery bags into the trunk and pile themselves into the car.

Sally reminds Mike that they've promised to show Ginger the photos they just picked up. Ginger has been carrying Charlotte's camera everywhere, documenting the rites of the past week.

"Yeah, we'll stop in on the way home," says Mike. "There are some really sweet ones of you and Wayne, Sal." He holds up the envelope. "Actually, we're *all* in here and we're *all* gorgeous!"

"Impossible," Wry teases. "*This* ugly lot?"

"It's magic." Elaine closes her eyes to see Charlotte swaying up the hill, bare feet in the grass and the wind playing with her hair.

POPPIES BLOOM IN SPRINGTIME

Erin Pitkethly

Poppy hesitated before opening the envelope. It had been sitting on the kitchen table for three days. Her roommate Adrian was nagging her about it that morning. He had asked her why she hadn't opened it and she couldn't say. She had answered impulsively, "If Julia has something to say to me, I'd like to hear it from her, not in a letter."

"Maybe it's not a letter," Adrian had responded. "Maybe it's an invitation. To an opening. Of an art thing-a-ma-jig." Adrian was from Argentina and was still working on his English. He had learned the word "thing-a-ma-jig" a few weeks back and now used it for any word he didn't know in English. He preferred this to anglicizing Spanish words.

"Art *exhibit*," Poppy had filled in for him.

It was true that the envelope looked too formal to be a letter. Maybe it *was* an invitation to an art exhibit. Probably in Vancouver where Julia now lived. If it were out west then it would be just a token gesture. An apology for not having returned her calls. Julia surely knew that Poppy was not going to go all the way to Vancouver for an opening. Not after two years of being ignored. A few years ago Poppy would have dropped everything and been there to support her. But not now. And what if the art show were in Toronto? Poppy couldn't excuse herself from an event in her own city. She knew Julia was having some success out west. Maybe she was ready to come back home. And take on the Ontario College of Art and Design grads.

Over the years Poppy had encouraged Julia through her many down moments about not having been accepted at OCAD. Julia had always just assumed that's where she would go after high school. When she didn't get in she was at a loss. She had neglected (refused actually) to apply anywhere else, so she had to scramble to get in at another school. The University of Guelph had a last minute opening, so she enrolled in fine arts there. Poppy knew Julia always had a complex about not being at OCAD, the top art school in the country. And she definitely resented not being in a bigger city. She complained that she couldn't be inspired in such a small town atmosphere; that she was stuck at a school that prided itself on its agricultural program; that they offered "half a degree" (HAFA was a course in Hotel and Food Administration); that there were cows in the middle of campus; and that the closest thing to a bohemian atmosphere at Guelph was line dancing. The truth was there was a lot going on both at the university and in the city that she didn't even know about because she was so busy working on her art assignments. But Poppy kept her mouth shut. (Her lighter schedule as an English and Sociology major afforded her the luxury of time to explore). She knew that because Julia had grown up near Guelph, it would always seem dull to her. Poppy liked to think that she was partly responsible for any success Julia might achieve in the future. She had, on more than one occasion, unpacked Julia's bags as her friend threatened to quit school.

Poppy hesitated another moment and then started to

rip open the envelope. She wanted to read the contents before Adrian got home. She was hoping he might forget about it and she could avoid any further discussion. Her jaw was still hanging open when Adrian entered the apartment and looked over at her.

"Is everything OK?" he asked. "You look a bit pale." He walked over to her and leaned over her shoulder. "Is that the letter from your friend?"

"Yeah. Except it's not a letter. It's a wedding invitation. To a guy named *Francis*."

"Didn't you say she swore she would never get married? That it would rechain her creativity?"

"Restrain. Yeah…" Then looking up she added, "I told you that?" only half-listening for a response.

He shrugged his shoulders. "People changed," and turned to his bedroom. She didn't smile at his mistake. She didn't even notice he was gone.

When he emerged from his room ten minutes later she was still staring at the wall in front of her.

"You weren't in love with her honey, were you?"

"No."

"Not even a little bit?"

"God Adrian. How many times do I have to tell you? I'm straight. Has it ever occurred to you that maybe your so-called 'gay-dar' only works on males?" She heard the knife in her voice and felt badly. "I'm sorry. I'm just shocked. And what the hell is she doing inviting me to her damned wedding when she hasn't so much as called me for two years?"

"Maybe she was busy. You know, figuring out the male anatomy."

Poppy didn't register that he was trying to make a joke. "She's an artist. She had plenty of exposure to male anatomy in school."

"I'm sorry honey, but I got to tell you: you sound jealous to me."

"Well listen a little more closely. I'm not. I'm going for a run. If I'm not back in two hours, call the cops. Goodbye."

She went to her room, conscious that she was stomping off like an angry teenager. It wasn't Adrian's fault this was happening. He was just trying to be a friend. But sometimes he could be so damned nosy. She wished that she could afford a place on her own.

A run would help her sort things out. By the time she got back this would almost be behind her. Because there was one thing she knew already—she was not going to any damned wedding of Julia's.

That night she lay in bed wondering what she would wear. Maybe a short bias-cut dress that showed off her legs. (Wasn't it bias-cut that Adrian was always yammering on about?) Or something long and slimming? Maybe Adrian could do something for her. And what about a date? Oh god. A date. The invitation had been to "Poppy and date." How damned impersonal that Julia had no idea who she was dating. Of course then it would have said to Poppy and No one. Who could she bring? She didn't want to ask an ex. There weren't any that she was still talking to anyway, so that wasn't even an option. If only she had a brother. You could bring a brother as a date to a wedding couldn't you?

There was always Adrian. There's nothing like a gay man for a wedding date. At least that's what she thought "they" said. She had a vague recollection of seeing this as one of the points she had read in some stupid on-line article: "Top Ten Ways to Steal the Show at Your Best Friend's Wedding." Must have been from *Glamour* magazine or something equally trashy. She had to stop reading that crap during slow days at the office. But it was true. Adrian would dress well, be able to dance, wouldn't hit on her when drunk and would be polite. Plus he was cute and had that sexy accent. Adrian was a definite option.

By the morning Poppy had to admit that Adrian was the only option. But would he go? A room full of artists would offer him lots of opportunity to meet "potentials" as he called them. He loved to dance. He was single and had no social life to deter him. The open bar would likely seal the deal.

Adrian agreed. Poppy didn't even have to beg. She RSVP'd a yes. By mail.

It took her a few days to hit Adrian up for a dress. She didn't want to push her luck. She brought home some cheesies to put him in a good mood. It didn't take much convincing though he insisted he would need to have "complete artistic control."

"It's gonna be red and it's gonna be sexy."

Poppy sighed. "How about pale pink"

Adrian gave a haughty sniff of disapproval. Then he started to gush again, "No. It's *got* to be red. I have always dreamed of making a red dress for a beautiful girl named Poppy."

Poppy rolled her eyes at him. "Don't you think that's a bit of a cliché."

"Honey you are going to look so fabulous people won't even trip over that."

Must be a Spanish thing lost in translation Poppy thought.

She retreated to her room with her coffee. She couldn't complain. She was getting a date and a dress. The only things left were shoes and a gift. Surely she could manage those two on her own.

It was during first year of university that Poppy decided she no longer wanted to travel to England for Christmas. Not that year anyway and probably not for a few years to come. She was tired of having to spend hours on an airplane, being jet-lagged, and then bored to death by her stodgy old relatives. Their gray weather did nothing to help entice her. She wanted a white Christmas for once, even if she had to spend it alone. Her parents refused to change their plans. This didn't surprise her. They said that she was now an adult and if that was her decision, so be it, but they were going to continue spending Christmas in England with their families as they had always done. She imagined this was punishment for her not applying to any British universities as they had hoped she would. Oh well. She could use some time away from them. She felt like they suffocated her whenever she went home for the weekend, even though they were never really around.

She had planned to spend the holidays alone. It would be refreshing. Sort of Zen: quiet, contemplative. Then Julia heard of her plans. She insisted Poppy spend Christmas at her house. At "the farm" as she called it. Nothing Poppy said would dissuade her. Three days after her exams had finished, Poppy sat waiting in the front entrance of her large brick house. Julia's mother was going to pick her up. Julia had not said much about her family except that they had supported her decision to become an artist. This alone set them apart from Poppy's parents. They were both lawyers. They had pressured Poppy, their only child, to choose some sort of professional program, or at the very least pursue a PhD. Sometimes she wished for an overachieving sibling.

Both Martha and George picked up Poppy in an old station wagon. A *very* old station wagon. With fake wood paneling on the side of the sort that Poppy had not seen

since elementary school. They had just been to the airport
to "fetch an old friend" they said. Larry, the friend, was a
music producer that George had met during his time as a
folk musician. George bragged about the famous musicians
Larry had worked with until Martha told him to shut-up
already, that Poppy probably didn't know any of the old
codgers George was going on about anyway.

As they drove out of the city Poppy felt her stomach
tighten with the worry that she might not be able to last a
week with these people. They were much louder than her
parents. She really had envisioned spending a quiet week
before Christmas. When Julia had said "farm" and "in the
country" she had pictured herself surrounded by a white
silence of snow. And quiet evenings by a fireplace with
tea. That now seemed about as likely as Santa coming down
the chimney.

The house was quiet when they arrived. There was no
sign of Julia or any of the brothers Poppy had just recently
learned about. Martha brought Poppy to Julia's room. She
could have the guest room once Larry left she said. Back in
the kitchen there was still no Julia.

"Did you bring skates?" Martha corrected herself, "Or,
do you skate, I should ask first?"

"Uh, yeah, I skate. But I didn't bring them with me."

"I told Julia to mention it to you. I don't know how she
could have forgotten. It's the only thing she and her brothers
have done since she got back. What size are your feet?"

"Seven, seven-and-half."

"I've got a pair that are size eight. With a pair of wool
socks they'll probably do. If you want them. Maybe you'd
rather just veg on the couch."

Julia considered saying yes to the couch. She was tired,
but for no good reason. It felt like the jet-lag she was used

to when traveling to England. She took a deep breath. She didn't want to be a bore. There'd be lots of time for sleep. "I'll try the skates."

"They're figure skates. I hope that's OK. There are extra hockey sticks in the garage. Grab one before you head down to the pond."

The skates fitted fine. Martha lent Poppy some warm outdoor clothes and sent her down with a thermos of hot chocolate. Poppy took two hockey sticks with her, one left- and one right-handed. She trudged down the well packed snow path. She couldn't see the pond because of the trees but she could hear the players yelling and laughing.

She was nervous about meeting the brothers (she always felt uneasy around friends' siblings, especially brothers) and about playing hockey for the first time. Although she was athletic—she played varsity soccer and had nearly made the basketball team—she was not a strong skater. She felt her hands clam up in anticipation of the frustration and embarrassment. She knew her competitiveness would force her to try to keep up once she got on the ice. At least the soccer season was over so there would be no lectures from her coach if she broke her leg.

"Poppyyyyyy!" Julia yelled with uncharacteristic enthusiasm. "Get your butt over here. I need a sub. Got to quit smoking and drinking if I'm going to keep up with these guys."

Poppy smiled to herself. She always thought Julia forced herself to smoke just to take cultivate an artistic image.

Julia turned towards her brothers. "Poppy's an amazing athlete. She led the soccer team in goals this year."

Poppy winced. "Actually I was second. And I can't really skate. Anyone for ice soccer? Or maybe broomball?" She continued desperately, "Hot chocolate?"

"Poppy this is Jordan, the baby—he hates when I say

that, Chris the middleman and Matt, my twin. Hey Matt, remember that poem Mom used to always say. 'Poppies bloom in spring time all along the lane, Showers something something on the window pane.' I tried to tell it to Poppy last week. It came to me when I was totally drunk. Just came to me."

Poppy tried not to look surprised. Julia had never mentioned a twin. That seemed like a pretty big deal. It wasn't like just another brother or sister. At least not to Poppy anyway, who of course had no experience with siblings to go by. You never knew with Julia though. She probably acted like it was no big deal just to be different.

Poppy smiled and said "Hi." She was about to say "I've heard so much about you," as her parents had coached her, but reconsidered. It was not only stuffy it was completely untrue. She had only just found out about Julia's siblings the week before Christmas. Instead she continued, "But, uhm, seriously, I think I might just play the role of ref for a bit, till I get my ice legs. I was going to say 'back' but I've never really had them. My parents are British. They don't skate. A neighbour's Dad taught me how one winter. Then they moved away. I think I was nine. So it's been a while."

Poppy felt like she was blabbering. She sized up the brothers nervously. They *seemed* to be listening through the steam rising from their hot chocolate. She felt awkward. She bent down to unlace her boots.

"There's a bench over there," Julia said, pointing to a pile of snow on the edge of the rink which had been packed to form a long seat.

Poppy crossed the pond precariously and put on the skates. She wished that she had opted for the couch up at the farmhouse now. At least then she would have gotten to know everyone before she had to skate in front of them.

Julia noticed the pained look on Poppy's face. "Don't

worry Poppy. We're not playing for chores, like we used to. You can be on Matt's team. Did I ever tell you that he plays hockey for U of G?"

Were the surprises never going to end? Not only did she have a twin, but he went to the same school that they did. Poppy wondered if Julia had spent the first semester pretending to be someone else. She felt nervous again about spending the week at the farm. Trapped. Julia read her face.

"Matt and I had an agreement to avoid each other. I didn't want to go to the same University as him, but when we both ended up at Guelph we decided to pretend we weren't at the same school. So we wouldn't use each other as a crutch, ya know." She shrugged.

Poppy could see that the brothers were getting restless standing around. "We can play two on one if you guys want to go to the house to talk," Jordan said impatiently.

Poppy stood up. "Well I'm all laced up. I might as well give this a try." She wobbled across to the opposite snow bank. "My biggest problem is that I can't stop, but I guess I can just glide into the snow here." She headed to grab a stick. "I don't know which hand to use."

Chris laughed. "This is sort of like coaching squirts again." Julia gave him a fierce glare. "I just mean that they don't know which handed they are."

"Well don't just stand there like an idiot, tell her what you tell them." He looked at her blankly. "About how to figure it out."

"We line them up and have them try shooting and passing both ways. We watch them and whatever looks the best and feels most comfortable they go with. I did have one kid switch after a year once."

Poppy tried it out. She decided to shoot right and joined the game. As best she could.

The week flew by. By the end Poppy was used to the raucous meals, the yelling to each other through the house, the stereo blasting in the middle of the afternoon. She didn't know if she'd be able to stand the staid silence in her parents' house the following week. She was relieved when they called to say they were going to be in England an extra ten days. An elderly aunt had passed away and they were helping with funeral arrangements and legalities. Of course Poppy could have returned home as planned. She certainly didn't need her parents to be there. But when Martha asked if she'd like to stay on, she heard the word "yes" before she'd even considered her answer.

That year Poppy returned for spring break (her parents were both busy with work and wouldn't have seen her anyway), for Easter (her parents were in Savannah, Georgia) and then for a few weeks that summer. She went to the farm for most school breaks for the next three years. Eventually the guest room became hers. After all, Martha pointed out, she *was* at the farm as much as Matt or Julia. Sometimes more. In her fourth year she spent Christmas at the farm even though Julia was in England finishing a semester there. By that time she considered Matt as much of a friend as Julia. She had a lot more in common with him, since they both had the pressure of juggling school and sports.

When Poppy lost touch with Julia, she felt she lost not just one friend, but two. And a family. For a while she was most angry with Matt. Julia was flighty and unreliable so Poppy wasn't surprised by her disappearance. But there was no reason *he* couldn't have called her. She once complained about this to a group of co-workers over lunch. One of the men had said that guys just weren't like that. They didn't keep in touch the way women did, with birthday cards and phone calls and all that shit. That's what he had said: "and all that shit." Poppy had thought, and all *what* shit? Still talking to someone was a waste of time when you live in different cities?

And what about Martha and George, she sometimes wondered? They had always referred to her jokingly as "the responsible daughter we never had." Or sometimes, because of her name, "the love child we never had." Maybe they *were* just flaky ex-hippies, like Matt always said. That's how she tried to think of them now. It was easier. Still, the year her parents went to live in England, Poppy found she missed Julia's family more than her own.

A month before Julia's wedding Adrian returned from work and danced into the apartment. He was grinning so widely that Poppy thought he was trying to be funny.

"What's wrong with *you*? You whiten your teeth or something?"

"Ha. Ha. Very funny. I'm going to Paris! I won that young designer's award. I leave next month."

"Congratulations! That's awesome! Do they pay for everything? Including a companion? I could be your chaperone in gay Paree!"

"Unfortunately it's just me going." He sighed, "There are parties, and fashion shows . . . and god, *the shopping*. Once I'm there I get to pick the models for my show. It's the real thing baby. I think we're the day before Versace.

Poppy winced. "You're not taking my dress with you are you?"

"To wear to the awards ceremony?" He didn't wait for an answer. "Now that I think of it, it would be a nice addition to the collection. Can I take it?"

"Well really it *is* yours."

"Especially since you haven't paid me for the material yet."

"Oh shit, sorry. Here I'll write you a cheque right now."
She looked in her briefcase for her cheque book. "When do
you leave?"

"May twelfth."

Great, I'll have the apartment to myself Poppy thought
as she wrote the cheque. Her hand froze. "Shit, shit, shit."

"Don't worry about it. I stole some of your energy bars—
they taste like crap, by the way—you know, to make up for
the interest."

"No. It's not that. You're going to miss the wedding.
I'll have no date. And worse, I'll have to call Julia and tell
her I have no date." What was she going to do? She could
always just say she was sick and not go. Migraines. She
had done it at work. She realized she had just sounded like
a spoiled child. "Ya know what? It's no big deal. I've been
meaning to call her anyway."

"So I guess I can't take the dress."

"If you want it, I'll go buy something else. I'm not sure
I could pull that red number off anyway. Especially without
a date. And I can't find shoes to wear. So take it."

He looked at her sympathetically. "I couldn't." He
stared at her feet. "I'll find you shoes. To make up for
leaving you dry and high. What size are you?"

"Seven and a half."

Poppy could feel the tension building in her body. Her
shoulders felt like cement. This is ridiculous, she thought.
It's not a big deal. She repeated to herself, it's no big deal.
Deep breaths. She forced herself to take deep breaths. She
retreated to her room to regain composure but felt worse.
She realized she would only feel better by calling Julia. Like
admitting to a crime, she would feel relief to get this off her
chest. But there was no point trying to find another date.
That was the whole reason she was taking her gay
roommate in the first place. There was no alternative.

"Julia, it's me, Poppy. How are you?"

"Poppy! I'm great! How are you? Where have you been?"

"Where have I been? Where the hell have you been?" Poppy realized this sounded harsher than she would have liked. Julia seemed not to notice.

"Here out west. But we're moving back east. To Montreal or Toronto. We haven't decided. So you got my invitation. I guess you changed apartments and I lost you for a while. I never did have your parents' number. When I didn't hear from you I just assumed you were too busy to keep in touch…. You know. Everybody always says they're so busy. Blah, blah, blah. Anyway, I really wanted you at my wedding so I tracked you down. Your number's not listed and neither is your parents'. It wasn't easy. I had somebody hand deliver the invitation to your parent's house and just hoped they still lived there."

"Really? But I got it in the mail. My mom must have mailed it to me. She never even mentioned it. Typical. She probably got her secretary to do it."

"How are your parents?"

"The same. Busy. And yours?"

"They're great. Happy to have all the kids out of the house, at least during the school year."

"And Matt?"

"He's OK now. You knew about his accident?"

"*No.*"

"He had a motorcycle accident. God it's been over two years now. He's walking again. Actually running now, I think. It was really hard for a while. You know how active he was. He lost his job, his girlfriend. He did his rehab at the farm for a year. But he's back to work now. It happened the summer after we graduated. No. The summer after that.

I tried to get a hold of you but I couldn't reach you."

Poppy felt a knot in her stomach. "Oh shit. You know what? That's when my roommate had an ex-boyfriend stalking her. We had to change phone numbers twice. I totally forgot about that." She paused to think about how everything had changed. "I feel so bad for Matt. Say hi to him for me, okay? And tell him if I had known, I would have come to visit. I just didn't hear from you guys so I thought you didn't want to... I don't know." She stopped. There was too much emotion in her voice. "Like you said, everybody's so busy. Anyway. The reason I'm calling is that my date can't come to your wedding. He has to go to Paris. For a fashion show. That sounds so phony. But it's true. Maybe I'll photocopy his plane ticket so people will believe me. It's not like he's my boyfriend or anything. So put me down for one person instead of two."

"Do you want to go with Matt?"

Poppy was surprised by this offer. "Sure, but don't you think you better ask him first? Yeah, of course. I'd love to."

"He'd really like to see you. I mean, he'll see you at the wedding anyway. But I'm sure he'd rather spend more time with you, ya know. I'll call him tonight and get back to you."

"Julia?"

"Yes."

"Can he still skate?"

"I think that's this winter's project."

"Tell him I want to see him on the ice."

"I don't know. He's pretty self-conscious."

"Do you remember when you first got me on the pond at the farm?"

Julia guffawed into the phone. "How could I forget? But you got better."

"Tell him I'll meet him on the ice."

"What about the wedding?"

"I'll see him there too. But I'll only go to the wedding with him if he promises me a date on the ice next winter."

"You drive a hard bargain."

"Tell him poppies might bloom in spring time but door mat's come out for the winter."

"Ha. He'll like that. He needs a bit of a kick in the butt anyway I think."

"Thanks Julia."

"For what."

"For finding me." Poppy laughed at herself, feeling corny. "And for finding me a date."

M^AGELLAN

Heidi Reimer

She struggled through a tangle of crystallized branches and stopped to tug the black toque further over her ears. The toque was old, and full of the little balls that old things get, and sometimes new things if you didn't pay enough for them. Ugly, too, but this was the bush; in the bush ugly didn't matter. Unless you were a hoity-toity up from Southern Ontario, matching ski suits, hats, gloves, yeah whatever. A real bush girl just dug through her closet and yanked on whatever mismatched and ancient outerwear she discovered. As long as it was warm. Away you go. Bush tromping.

Despite the frigid temperature, she craved this tromp today. She needed movement in her legs and clear air to her head. She might keep going until she froze.

The producer from Toronto was no doubt the type who wore matching stuff. Well she'd see. He wasn't expected till four in the afternoon. Gave her plenty of time to get home, sit at the kitchen table with a cup of mint tea. Brood a while, maybe play. Change her clothes.

She was almost home when the strange car crawled, tentative, past her. A Camry, dark blue, new. The kind that never appeared on the back roads. She slung it a scowl and continued her trudge toward the house. A ways up, near the S curve, the Camry braked, maneuvered a multi-point turn, crept back toward her. She stopped. An automatic window glided down.

"Excuse me?" An angular face, carefully razored, peered at her from beneath a copse of black hair.

"Yes."

"I think—I think I'm lost?"

"Yes."

"I'm looking for the home of Ms. Laine Scoffield."

Hell. Well. The producer was early. A whole hour.

"Would you know her?"

She regarded him, measured. "Yeah, I know her."

The creased face released itself into a grin. "I suppose everybody knows everybody around here, eh?"

She shrugged.

"Do you think you could, uh, direct me?"

"Follow me." She crunched across the snow-caked gravel, and he shifted into drive and inched after her. Great. Why the hell was he an hour early? And she in her bush grubbies. Toronto people think Sudbury is up near the Arctic Circle, that's why; he probably left a week ago to make it here.

He turned after her into the driveway. She clumped to the side door and banged the snow from her Cougars. The engine died. Gripping a black leather briefcase, the man slunk from the driver's seat. "This is where she lives?"

"Yup."

"I—I'm early, she might not expect me yet."

Nope, she doesn't. "Might as well come in anyway, I'll grab her for you."

"You're sure it's okay to...walk into her house like this?"

Her glasses fogged as the warm air hit them.

"Everybody knows everybody around here."

She kicked her boots off and left him standing in the entrance, fiddling with the clasp on his briefcase. Her bedroom was through the kitchen and up a string of stairs. She climbed them with a hurry that annoyed her. He could wait. She didn't care about any of this. They were wasting their time; it was their fault for insisting they send someone.

She tossed her old coat on the bed, yanked off the toque, frowned into the mirror at the hair static-clung to her head. In the bathroom across the hall she ducked her head under the tap, squirted mousse liberally onto her palm and massaged it through her hair. Better. The Julia Roberts look, Frank used to say. Except her smile wasn't as wide.

So she wrote songs. She'd always written songs. She entered a contest, she won, she got the money. Great. It didn't mean she needed a guy who couldn't find his way on a dirt road coercing her to make an album of them.

In her room she changed into a red sweater and flowing black skirt. Not too dressy, but professional enough, feminine enough. She discarded her glasses and worked a flimsy contact into each eye. In front of the mirror, foundation on her thawing face, blush, bit of red lipstick.

As if someone live at her kitchen table would make a difference when their letters and phone calls hadn't. Especially this guy—he didn't seem the sort to persuade himself of anything, forget persuading her.

In the entrance she smiled and stretched her hand toward him. "Sorry to keep you waiting."

"Not at all." He smiled now, more confident, more in his forte than he'd been wandering country roads asking directions of bush girls. "I'm pleased to meet you, Ms. Scoffield."

"Call me Laine."

"And I'm Andrew. Andrew Newman."

A minion. He wasn't on the letterhead.

"I had trouble finding you. Your friend kindly directed me."

Three cheers for mousse, contacts, and lipstick. "That was me."

"That was—you?"

"Yes, but you're early. I wasn't ready, I had to buy time." He was at a loss; she smirked as it showed on his face. "Come in."

She led him to the kitchen. "What can I get you to drink?"

"Coffee?"

"No."

"No?"

"I only have mint tea."

"Uh—sure. That would be fine."

Out of his element again. Did they all lose their bearings the minute they stepped from a skyscraper? She filled the kettle, flicked the burner to max, settled a teabag into her chipped Laura Ashley teapot. Gift from Frank, from his trip to England, after it was over but they were still trying to be friends.

They talked about the bitter cold and his drive up, until the kettle boiled and she poured the steaming water over the peppermint and carried it with mugs to the table.

"So"—might as well take charge, he wasn't—"you folks want me to record a collection of my songs."

"Yes."

"You want to turn me into—who, Joni Mitchell?"

"How about Laine Scoffield?"

"I'm already Laine Scoffield."

Her guitar lay across the table, she'd been playing before her walk. She picked it up, for security, hugged it lightly like it was human. It *was* human, sort of, his name was

Magellan.

His pitch spanned two hours. She timed it by the waning sun, cold in the pale afternoon sky. He gutted his briefcase, displayed charts, explained terms, deciphered a contract. Appealed. It had been foolish, of course, to let them send someone; she even had to switch shifts at work for it.

"Listen." His spiel lulled, and she grabbed the opening. "When I was sixteen, yeah, this would have been great. This was my dream, to give my life to music. My parents and teachers—everyone—said nobody succeeds at that. They wanted me to be a, I don't know, teacher or lawyer, I don't remember. Nurse. Know what I became?" She felt the sneer on her face, could not check it. "Cashier at K-mart."

"Do you find it fulfilling?"

She glared. "I do music in the evenings. That is my fulfillment."

"But nobody hears it."

"I play at parties sometimes."

"That's like a writer whose sole public venue is a poem in the odd birthday card."

He was frustrated. She arched her eyebrows at him, intrigued by this new passion, and said nothing.

"You're an artist not pursuing your art," he said. "You can't be happy."

She thought of scraping her chair back from the table, telling him this was enough. Nice meeting you. Don't forget your briefcase.

"It's just that, you have so much to offer—"

"So much for you to exploit."

"Is that your fear?"

"Andrew, the music wouldn't be mine anymore. It'd be yours. Your company's. You would own me, and own my songs."

"You would retain the right to—"

"I'm not talking about what's on paper. I'm talking about how it would feel to me."

She slouched deeper into her chair. She didn't have to tell him the truth. This business-suited, briefcased, "you would retain the right" producer's minion, who thought he knew if she was happy.

"Your music is important to you."

Duh.

With one finger she traced the spout of the Laura Ashley teapot. The plump body, the handle, the lid with its delicate painted flowers. The chip where she had hurled the lid at the wall, in hatred at herself for letting fear, and family expectations, and practicality rule her heart.

"I had a man once," she said, "who I was going to marry. There were differences we couldn't reconcile, and in my head I couldn't see it working. I still loved him. It might have worked. I have no decent relationships with my family. I have no education and a job I hate. I have this house, where I live alone. I have my bush trails, and Magellan. And my music. I have my music, Andrew, and I would like to keep my music."

He regarded her, his eyes ridiculously soft. He was a stranger, why was she telling him this? She looked away from his eyes, at the darkness creeping over the yard, and knew it was because he was a stranger, and he didn't matter. He didn't know her or anyone she knew, and within the hour he would creep into his slick car and drive back to Toronto and she'd never see him again.

"Are you afraid?" he asked.

She felt like shaking him. Of course she was afraid. Saying yes to Andrew Newman would be territory unknown. It would be rousing the dreams her father pounded into the grave while she was still a child. Facing the regret of what her life had become. More, it would be the attempt to work beyond that regret, and turn it around, and that was scarier than leaving it be. She could play to herself in her quiet house, and keep a fat binder of her songs, and process her life through words and music. And she could be, if not content, reconciled.

"I think, Mr. Newman, you'd better go."

He looked at her like his heart would break. What was it to him? He would lose points with his superiors, she supposed, but it shouldn't be life and death. She rose, briskly, and fetched his coat from the closet. He shrugged into it, reassembled his briefcase, said nothing. Perceptive. He knew she wanted him to say nothing, and he knew if he said something it would do no good.

She slipped a coat on to walk him to his car. The ice air slapped her as she stepped outside behind him. The temperature had dropped further; even she, used to it, gasped at the sting of cold.

"I hope you don't regret making the long trip for nothing."

"No. It was good to meet you." He slid onto his frozen seat, shoved the key into the ignition with a leather-gloved hand. She felt a twinge of desperation. This interlude, with this stranger from Toronto, offering a chance to change her life—offering fulfillment of dreams—had been a sort of dream itself. She knew all along she wouldn't accept, but she let him come because she wanted to think what if. She wanted to know she *could*. She wanted for one afternoon something different in the monotone of her life. Already it was over.

"You'll want to let it run a while, to warm up."

But the engine refused to turn over. He tried again—a third time, a fourth.

"This freaking cold," he said.

She nodded. "Don't suppose you've got a block heater?"

"A what?"

"Didn't think so."

He got out and fiddled under the hood, returned to the wheel and tried the key again. She shivered beside him, the cold gusting up her skirt and around her bare head.

"It won't start," she said.

His shoulders slumped against the seat.

She said, "I'll plug my car in, in a couple hours it'll run. I can drive you to your hotel, at least."

"What about my car?"

"We could worry about it in the morning."

He left his briefcase in the entrance. She had spaghetti sauce in the fridge; she figured, a couple hours, she might as well feed him, and she put a pot on for pasta. She sat down at the table, caressed Magellan absently with one hand, looked at Andrew Newman. Like two lovers whose fight was over, and lost by both of them, there was nothing more to say.

I'm sorry, she wanted to tell him. Tell him, tell herself. Later, when he left, would she hurl the whole teapot this time?

Instead, "Do you play?" she asked.

"A...a little."

She could swear that was a blush.

"Strum something for me?"

She offered Magellan. He eyed her, uncertain, furtive, then grasped the neck of Magellan and swung him up into his arms. His fingertips were soft; if he played he had not played lately. He ran a hand across the mahogany, and, with a strange expectancy, she watched.

Slowly the fingers of his left hand closed over a barred E; his right settled on the strings spanning the hole of

Magellan. He played. Simple at first, but gradually more intricate, a song she didn't know. Perhaps he'd written it. She leaned forward in her chair, smiled. He kept playing, and she picked a note and hummed, then turned it into singing, and he smiled back. She made up words, and he added a harmony in a strong tenor that shivered up her back. Uncannily, he followed the melody she was creating, read her words before they left her mouth. His fingers flew along Magellan's strings, limber, dexterous.

Magic.

She read his eyes then. It was himself he meant—"you're an artist not pursuing your art: you can't be happy." He didn't want to spend his life persuading others to chase their dreams. He wished he had the opportunity she was turning down, wished to see her grasp it, to live it vicariously through her. He understood her fear; he'd succumbed to it himself. Those uncalloused fingers never played anymore.

She sang, tenderly, as his rich voice mingled with hers, inhabiting the kitchen. His recording company did not know his talent. They had no idea—no idea—how good his voice on an album would sound with hers.

A forgotten sensation of thrill assailed her gut, so that for a moment her voice almost trembled.

The song was complete. They knew it at the same time, uncued. The words ended, the finger-picking on Magellan lingered, softened, died. Finished.

He raised his eyes to hers, glowing. Knowing.

She smiled.

GÖDEL'S THEOREM

F. G. Paci

Eva Bertulli Schmidt sat on the beach chair in her pink bikini and looked over the water. Adjusting her sunglasses against the glare, she focused on the deserted island in the middle of the bay. Densely forested, it had rolling hills and a barren rocky shoreline. Beyond the island the expanse of Lake Superior merged with the blue sky.

It was close to five o'clock on a warm Friday in the first week of June. Though the water would be extremely cold, she was waiting to take her customary June dip before supper.

She closed her eyes and stretched back on her chair. It had been an exhausting week. And it wouldn't get any easier this evening with her boys coming up to the camp for the weekend.

She was going to break the news to her sons and father this evening during supper. Alone. Kurt, her husband, would come up to the camp tomorrow.

The sun felt good on her skin. Her mind, however, was too agitated for her to relax.

The slightest thing could disturb her. Just this morning, for example, she had almost lost it during her first period class.

She had left the room momentarily to do some photocopying. When she came back, a group of her senior students were seated in a ring in a heated debate about miracles. The rest of the class was listening. It was difficult enough getting seventeen year olds intensely interested in anything this early in the morning. She decided to listen as well.

Kids always amazed her by what they knew underneath their academic ignorance.

Kevin, her resident clown, had said, "Can God create a stone so heavy that even He can't lift it?"

Everyone had groaned.

And then one of the girls, Christina, a bright student with dark eyes and a big smile, had looked at her. "What do you think, Miss?"

She thought for a moment. "It's a variation of the Liar's Paradox. Someone comes up to you and says, I'm a liar. Is his statement true or false? Well, it just goes in a vicious circle, doesn't it? It's a paradox. It has no correct answer. Life is full of paradoxes. Ultimately we live in the prison house of language."

Christina, crestfallen, said, "You don't believe in God, do you, Miss?"

"It's a public school," she said. "I'm not going to foist my religious beliefs—or lack thereof—on you."

"Can't you be honest with us, Miss?" Christina said. "You're close to retirement, aren't you? What do you care what they think?"

Eva had felt the cold cynical eyes of the class on her.

At that point her mind had gone into gridlock. Only a few seconds later did she realize a few tears had slipped down her cheeks.

It wasn't easy breaking out of old habits. Avoiding

difficult questions. Being ruthlessly honest with oneself. Escaping from the prison house of self-deception. But she knew she'd have to do so soon.

"It's not too late," she said out loud. "It can't be too late."

Sitting on the beach chair, Eva thought about what she'd say to her two sons. It's not too late, she'd say. Even though she was just past fifty. Even though the years had nestled themselves in every fold and wrinkle of her skin. In every age spot and varicose vein. In every deposit of cellulite on the backs of her legs.

When she was young she had thought she'd cut through any Gordian Knot and live out her life in spite of paradox. Life wasn't meant to be known but to be lived. To dedicate oneself to a noble ideal and to push ahead regardless of the sacrifices. This was during the years when she had her fill of university with its endless babble of theories which amounted to nothing.

After getting her degree and teacher's certificate, she was ready to tackle the world. Her eyes shone bright with expectation and challenge. To be independent. To show her family she could do it on her own. To instil the love of literature and thinking in the young.

She had plenty of offers to stay in the big bad city. There were enough boys. With their desires planted firmly in their eyes. And their endearing fumbling attempts to get into her pants. She was a beauty back then. Lithe and graceful. With long blond hair and sparkling eyes. Everyone did a double-take when she told them she was Italian. They called her the blond *paesan*. It had been the era of free love and revolution and mind-altering drugs. She could've easily accepted one of these boys, some of whom had gone on to become corporation lawyers, politicians, doctors, and executives. But no, she loved her hometown too much. She loved the unspoiled beauty of the northern forests. The Lake Superior shore with its wind-swept fir trees. The clean air. And her family. Her close-knit Italian family.

One's family was the most important thing in life, her father never ceased to tell her. *La famiglia*. Governments could topple. Wars could come and go. Foreigners could invade the country. Natural disasters could wipe out villages and towns. But the family remained intact. A bulwark. Inviolate and sacrosanct amidst the turmoil and fickleness of the world. Though her father's analogies were more fitting to a businessman.

Her family had immigrated to the Soo back in the thirties. Her father had run a grocery store on James Street during the heyday of the West End. Later he had become a city councillor. She had grown up in the West End, Little Italy, knowing her dad, Lino Bertulli, was a respected businessman and one of the city's favourite sons.

Lino had bought this camp north of Batchawana way back in the sixties for a pittance. It had natural beach sand, a shallow inlet of water, and was only about an hour's drive north from the city. He had been the first to build a camp. Others had come shortly afterwards to fill the bay with cottages. Now it was worth five to ten times its original price. Lino was in the house right now preparing his favourite dish, veal scallopini. Her sons, Jamie and John, would be there any minute.

Her mom had died five years ago of leukemia. She had not been the only one in the family to contract the disease. There had been a cousin and aunt. Her brother Daniel, who was three years younger and worked in Administration at the steel plant, had become paranoid he'd get it next. His wife Melanie had left him a few years ago and taken the kids back to Erie, Pennsylvania.

Eva shook her head. Daniel had always been the worrywart. It was so ironic.

It must've been five-thirty when she stepped into the water. Her body shivered. Her feet manoeuvred over the weeds. When she was up to her knees, she dove in and felt the slam of the cold take her breath away.

How many times had she taken a swim in these waters? How many times had she gone skinny dipping in the evening dusk? Made love with Kurt in the water with the full moon glistening off the bobbing waves?

They had raised their sons here. They had spent almost every weekend and most of the summer holidays at her father's camp. They had gone up to Wawa often and a few times around the north shore of Superior to Thunder Bay, exploring every nook and cranny of the bushland and shoreline. They had gone deep into the bush towards Agawa canyon and Chapleau and Timmins, on canoe trips and hiking expeditions. In winters they skied. Downhill and cross-country.

It was a wonderful life. Her ideals had taken a backseat to raising her two boys who had grown up with a deep love for the outdoors.

Jamie was twenty-five. After getting his degree, he had lived in Austria and then France, where he got involved with bicycle tours in Provence. He was a handsome outgoing young man, with her blond hair and Kurt's thin build. He had to beat the girls away. John, on the other hand, was dark and introverted. Two years younger than Jamie, he was thinking of going to teacher's college like her. John was more like Kurt, who was quiet and reserved. Kurt, who had come from Austria as a young man to work at the steel plant as an engineer.

She and Kurt had taken the boys to Austria often to see his folks who lived in an Alpine village. So, when Vice Principal Mark Biagini had approached her to organize a school trip to the Alps, she had chosen Innsbruck, which she knew like the back of her hand. She and Mark had taken a group of ten kids who were expert skiers. They had gone on excursions to Munich and Vienna. Then south, past the Stubai Glacier to the Dolomites in Italy. To Bolzano and Brescia and Milan. The kids found the Alps breathtaking. They had stayed at small chalets and large ski resorts. Mark had just recently separated from his wife. He needed the trip, he said, to regain his bearings and get on with his life. They had spent more than one evening discussing what they'd do upon retiring. What they had put off to raise their families. They shared many interests. Mark and his brother were going to buy a villa in Tuscany. He wanted to paint. His life was just beginning, he said.

He had inspired her. They had hit it off.

After ten minutes or so in the water, she hurried back to the shore, wrapped herself in a towel, and ran back to the camp. It was a two-storey clapboard building, with a covered verandah and four bedrooms, surrounded by birch trees and just a few yards from the dirt road that came from the highway. She noticed the family SUV was parked beside her compact. The boys had arrived.

Inside Lino was standing at the stove, working on the vegetables while the veal was simmering in wine sauce and mushrooms. John was on one of the sofas playing solitaire on the coffee table. Jamie was upstairs in his bedroom.

"You're crazy, Mom," John said. "It's too cold yet."

"She always has to be the first in the water," Lino said, without turning around. "Your mom was always like that as a little girl. Absolutely fearless. Why, I remember once at the pool hall on James Street—"

"Dad, please," she said. "Not that story again. They've heard it a hundred times. I just took a little dip. The really fearless guys are the polar bear swimmers who jump into a hole in the ice in the middle of winter."

"She's so modest, isn't she?" John said.

"All the Bertullis are modest," Lino said. "We don't have to flaunt our talents. They speak for themselves."

Eva rubbed her hair vigorously with the towel and gave out a laugh.

"Who's the best chef in the Soo?" she said.

"Not to mention Batchawana and Pancake Bay," John said, smiling and looking at his grandfather.

"Okay, okay," Lino said, turning around. "A little self-promotion doesn't hurt anyone."

For all his seventy-five years, her father was still a fine specimen of a man. His movements were slower and he had a definite hunch in his bearing, but he was still trim, with a full head of hair, which he dyed a deep black, and lean features. Wearing tan slacks and his slippers, with his blue polo shirt, he presented the image of a self-assured doyen of the family. Jokingly they called him Rinaldo Reagan, after the American president who, as far as she was concerned, had managed to stitch his brand of conservatism with the needle of a suave empty-headedness.

Later they were all seated at the kitchen table. The sun was low outside on the verandah and the beech trees darkened the backyard. Through the trees she could see the water.

"These are a couple of bottles from my best year," Lino said, indicating the two bottles of homemade wine on the table. "Let's make a toast to the boys. To their futures."

Eva drank up and looked at her boys.

"*Nono*," Jamie said, "there's no wine in all of France that's as good as this."

Lino kept his head down. "It was made the year your grandmother passed away," he said. His voice had collapsed. "One of life's little ironies, I suppose. Or maybe

I just think it's my best year so I can preserve her memory a little longer."

"Dad," Eva said. "Please. Not tonight."

Her father looked up from his plate and gave her a dead-eye stare.

"Thanks for all you've done, Eva," he said. "I would never have got through it without you."

"Don't mention it, Dad."

"You're just like her," he said. "In so many ways."

Eva hung her head and fell silent.

"Do you regret anything, Eva?" he said. "In your life, I mean."

"I don't know. I'd have to think about it."

"What's there to think about?"

"Dad, the boys don't want us reminiscing."

John, who was eating heartily, looked at her. "Sure, we'd like to hear, Mom. We wanna hear what you regret in your life. What you would've done different."

"My life's not over yet," she said.

"You know what we mean," Jamie said.

She paused and bit her lip. Oddly what came to mind was this morning's debate in her classroom. And her mention of the Liar's Paradox. If she regretted anything in her life, then she was saying she would've done it differently. But if she had done anything different, she wouldn't be where she was now, with her two boys. There were no half measures. It was either all or nothing. One had to accept all the consequences. Her mistakes and weaknesses as well as her triumphs and strengths.

Eva thought she had a pretty good life. But was it the best possible life she could've had? Had she compromised too much? Had she accomplished all that she had set out to do when she was the fearless young lady of the West End? Or had she settled for the easy course? Had she been

218 F. G. Paci

too much the martyr like her mother? Did she have the guts to experience the grand passions before it was, in fact, too late?

How could she possibly know? If she was the liar?

"Mom, what do you regret?" Jamie said.

She looked at him. "I regret nothing."

"I wish I had your balls," Lino said.

She looked at her father and smiled. "Is that what it seems?"

"Mom, why did you insist we come to the camp tonight?" John said.

"I have some news for you," she said. "But not now. I'll wait till after the meal."

"Why isn't dad here?" Jamie said.

"He knows already," she said. "I wanted to tell you guys alone."

All three men looked up from their eating and stared at her.

Eva resumed her eating. The veal tasted good. It went down with the homemade wine made the year her mother had died.

It was all a paradox. And she knew there were no ultimate answers. All she could do was dive into the water and let it take her breath away.

Notes on Contributors

KATHY ASHBY, Bracebridge, has published in the *Toronto Star, Canadian Writers' Journal, Scrivener's Pen Literary Journal, Artichoke Magazine, Muskoka Magazine* and *Canadian Women Studies*. She produced three narratives aired on CBC Radio One's programme Outfront. In October 2004 she was nominated for a YWCA, Woman of Distinction Award in the Arts Category.

DAVID BURTT, Wellington, NZ (South River and Lively), has worked as a tree-planter and canoe guide in the woods of Northern Ontario and Manitoba. Since receiving his MA in English in 2003 he has travelled, living most recently in Wellington, New Zealand. He has not been previously published.

VERA CONSTANTINEAU, Copper Cliff, is a journalist whose writing has been published in daily and weekly newspapers, magazines, and has aired on CBC radio's Regional and National broadcasts.

RICK COOPER, Sudbury, professor of English at Cambrian College, is past winner of the *Toronto Star* Short Story Contest for "The Pagoda."

SUSAN ELDRIDGE-VAUTOUR, Worthington, has not been previously published.

BARRY GRILLS, Field, chair of the Book and Periodical Council and a past chair of The Writers' Union of Canada, is the author of three cultural biographies on the lives of Anne Murray, Alanis Morissette, and Celine Dion.

COLIN HAYWARD, Garson, professor of theatre at Cambrian College, has published many travel stories and won several prizes for his short fiction. "Currency Exchange" was previously serialized on CBC Radio's Northern Writers Series. He is a past winner of the *Toronto Star* Short Story Contest.

TOMSON HIGHWAY, the French River area (and the French Riviera), is the acclaimed author of the novel *Kiss of the Fur Queen*, and the plays *The Rez Sisters*, and *Dry-Lips Oughta Move to Kapuskasing*, as well as being a classical pianist. He was named by *Maclean's* magazine as one of the 100 most important people in Canadian history. "Hearts and Flowers" first appeared in fall 2004 in *Our Story: Aboriginal Voices on Canada's Past*, published by Doubleday Canada, a Division of Random House of Canada Limited as a project of The Dominion Institute.

MARGO LITTLE, Gore Bay, a Manitoulin Island native, works as a freelance journalist for First Nations and mainstream newspapers and magazines. She has published *The Other Woman Was Lady Luck: True Stories from Monte Carlo to Casino Windsor* examining the impact of legalized gambling on Canadian family life. Her Northern Ontario tales have won numerous short story competitions. She is a founding member of the Sudbury Writers' Guild as well as founder of the Manitoulin Writers' Retreat.

BARBARA FLETCHER MACKAY, Wolfville, NS (Sault Ste. Marie), is former professor of theatre and drama therapy at

Concordia University. "Mabel's Kitchen" is her first published story.

ERIC MOORE, Sudbury, is a former CBC radio host, and winner of three short story competitions.

F. G. PACI, Toronto (Sault Ste. Marie), has published 11 novels since 1978, when *The Italians* came out. *Black Madonna* (Oberon,1982) is considered his most acclaimed novel. It is the story of a young Canadian woman who rejects her Italian background and abandons her old-fashioned Italian mother. Since 1990 he has published six novels in the Black Blood series. *Italian Shoes* (Guernica, 2002) is the fifth in the series. The sixth, *Hard Edge* (Guernica), was published in the spring of 2005. Another novel, *Losers* (Oberon), which came out in 2002, deals with marginalized students and the teachers who make a difference in their lives. He has also written about the struggles and triumphs of kids and their parents in minor league hockey in the novel *Icelands* (Oberon, 1999).

ERIN PITKETHLY, Corbeil, was a finalist in the Northern Ontario Poetry Competition in 2003, and won Sudbury's *Northern Life* Christmas Short Story Contest.

HEIDI REIMER, Wahnapitae, has had stories appear in a variety of print and online journals. "Magellan" was originally published in the Canadian Authors Association *Winner's Circle 9*.

MANSEL ROBINSON, Saskatoon (Chapleau), is a nationally known playwright whose plays include *Street Wheat, Ghost Trains, Downsizing Democracy* and *Spitting Slag* and have been produced in Ottawa, Kitchener, Edmonton, Saskatoon and Calgary. A book of short fiction and poetry, *Slag*, was published to acclaim in 1997. *Scorched*

Ice will premiere in Saskatoon in 2005. *Picking Up Chekhov,* directed by D. D. Kugler, was workshopped at the National Art Centre in June 2005 as part of On the Verge 2005, a Festival of New Play Readings, and will premiere at Alberta Theatre Projects playRites Festival in Calgary in 2006.

ARMAND GARNET RUFFO, Ottawa (Chapleau) is a member of the Fox Lake First Nation. He is the author of the acclaimed *Grey Owl: the Mystery of Archie Belaney* and *At Geronimo's Grave*, winner of the Archibald Lampman Poetry Award in 2002. His plays include an adaptation of *Grey Owl* and *A Windigo Tale*, winner of the CBC Arts Performance Showcase Award, which will appear as a feature film in 2006.

TISH P. SASS, Espanola, is a past "Judges' Choice" winner of the *Toronto Star* Short Story Contest for "After the Fall Comes Winter."

SUE SCHERZINGER, Sudbury, has had one of her stories air in CBC radio's Points North Northern Writer's Series.

LAURENCE STEVEN, Sudbury, is the publisher of Your Scrivener Press, as well as being Professor of English at Laurentian University and Director of Laurentian's Interdisciplinary Humanities MA in Interpretation and Values.

LOLA LEMIRE TOSTEVIN, Toronto (Timmins), nationally recognized poet (most recently *Site-Specific Poems*, 2004), critic, novelist, short story writer, and translator, is perhaps best known for *Frog Moon*, a novel of linked stories about growing up bilingual in Timmins. "The Iron Horse" is excerpted from *Frog Moon*, originally published by Cormorant Books in 1994.

NATALIE WILSON, North Bay, has published short fiction and poetry in a variety of journals. Her poems form one-third of the 1998 Your Scrivener Press collection *NeoVerse*, by Monique Chénier, Melanie Marttila, and Natalie Wilson.